3 9082 12... D0328791

SUBSTITUTE

CREATURE

SUBSTITUTE CREATURE

TALES FROM
LOVECRAFT
MIDDLE SCHOOL #4

By
CHARLES GILMAN

Illustrations by
EUGENE SMITH

QUIRK BOOKS
PHILADELPHIA

Library of Congress Cataloging in Publication Number: 2012953946

ISBN: 978-1-59474-640-6
Printed in China
Typeset in Bembo, Candida, and House MonsterFonts

Designed by Doogie Horner
Illustrations by Eugene Smith
Cover photography by Jonathan Pushnik
Cover model: Deanna Perlmutter
Production management by John J. McGurk
Lenticular manufactured by National Graphics, Inc.

Quirk Books
215 Church Street
Philadelphia, PA 19106
quirkbooks.com

10 9 8 7 6 5 4 3 2 1

This book
is for Julie

CHAPTER ONE

"Just five more m-m-minutes," Robert Arthur said.

"In five minutes we'll be dead," Glenn Torkells said. "We have to go *now*."

The outdoor temperature was barely twenty degrees. The boys were dressed in jeans and chorus robes but little else: no jackets, no hats, no gloves, no sneakers, no socks.

And they were trapped on a narrow ledge outside Lovecraft Middle School, four stories above the ground.

A freezing wind pinned them against the stone wall. Robert's right hand had found a crack in the mortar, the smallest of handholds, and he wedged his fingers inside.

"We can't just stand here," Glenn said.

"Someone will s-s-see us," Robert insisted. "We have to be pa-pa-patient.'

Glenn looked down—all the way down—but didn't see a single person. The boys were perched on the back wall of the school, high above the empty athletic fields. All of their classmates were indoors, attending a special Valentine's Day concert in the auditorium.

"This is our last chance," Glenn said. "If we wait any longer, we'll be too numb to move."

Robert worried the moment had already passed. His fingers and toes were tingling, as if his hands and feet had fallen asleep. Was it frostbite? Or hypothermia? Which was worse?

"Let's try yelling again," he suggested.

"It's no use," Glenn insisted.

The boys had already screamed themselves hoarse, but Robert hadn't given up. "J-j-just a few more tries," he said. "It'll warm us up."

So together they shouted *Help!* and *Please!* and

Somebody! and *Can anyone down there hear us?!?* but it was hopeless. No one could hear them. Their cries were lost beneath the blustery winds.

"We have to get to the balcony," Glenn said. "It's our only way out of this."

He was referring to the small railed patio on the side of the building. To reach it, the boys would need to follow the ledge around the corner of the school.

"What about the roof?" Robert suggested. The top of the building was maddeningly close, just inches beyond their fingertips. "What if you gave me a boost?"

Glenn shook his head. "I've seen you climb the ropes in gym class," he said. "You're not strong enough. Reaching the balcony is our only option."

"I won't make it," Robert said. "I'll fall."

"You *might* fall. But if you stay here—if you do nothing—you'll *definitely* fall. So what's it gonna be?"

Robert looked around for alternatives. At four stories high, the world seemed like it had turned to black and white; there wasn't a trace of color anywhere in

9

the sky. Just layers and layers of murky gray. The sun had vanished.

"All right," he decided. "Here goes nothing."

He eased his fingers from the crevasse and pressed both palms flat against the stones. Almost instantly, a fresh blast of wind whipped beneath his robe, blowing it up and over his head. Unable to see, Robert panicked. He reached out for Glenn, grabbing his shoulder, clinging to him until the wind settled down.

"Take it easy," Glenn said.

"I can't handle this," Robert told him.

"Yes, you can."

"No, I can't. I was okay when Professor Goyle turned into a winged demon. When Sarah and Sylvia Price turned into snake-women. When Howard Mergler turned into a giant fly-faced bug monster. All that crazy stuff, I could handle. Heck, I even fought back. But this ledge? At this height? With this wind? This is too much." Robert shook his head. "This is the worst."

For a few moments, neither boy said anything.

And then a fluffy white speck twirled out of the sky and landed on the tip of Glenn's nose.

A snowflake.

All around them, all at once, it was snowing.

"Things could always be worse," Glenn said.

CHAPTER TWO

Some kids might have trouble understanding how two boys could find themselves trapped on a narrow ledge outside their school and forty feet off the ground.

Of course, these same kids have probably never been trapped in their lockers by giant tentacled beasts. Or trapped in their bedrooms with boa constrictors. Or trapped underground with thousands of chirping and chattering insects.

But for Robert Arthur and Glenn Torkells, these kinds of near-death experiences were all just a regular part of seventh grade.

A few months earlier, the boys had discovered that

Lovecraft Middle School was constructed from the recycled remains of Tillinghast Mansion—a crumbling estate that was once home to the mad physicist Crawford Tillinghast. Because of a botched experiment, the mansion still existed in a parallel dimension; Robert and Glenn could pass from the school to the mansion and back again through hidden portals called "gates."

The boys soon learned that Tillinghast was capturing teachers and students, placing their souls in ceramic urns, and then using their flesh and hair as disguises for an army of bizarre monsters. The school was slowly being infiltrated by demons, snake-people, giant insects, and other ancient creatures summoned from distant dimensions.

Armed with this knowledge, Robert and Glenn went to school every day determined to stop Tillinghast and always expecting the worst. Yet nothing could have prepared them for the strange events of February fourteenth.

The day began with an announcement from the principal inviting all students to a surprise Valentine's

Day concert by the music department. As Robert followed his classmates into the auditorium, teachers gave out programs listing all the songs.

Glenn read the titles aloud in disbelief. "'Love Me Tender'? 'Eternal Flame'? 'You Are the Sunshine of My Life'?" He crumpled the program into a ball. "This is going to be torture!"

"Well, don't spoil it for the rest of us," said Karina Ortiz. "Robert and I are looking forward to it."

"Are you kidding me?" Glenn said, laughing. "Robert hates Valentine's Day even more than I do!"

Robert just shrugged. A year ago, he would have agreed with Glenn that Valentine's Day was a dumb holiday designed to sell overpriced chocolates. But since arriving in seventh grade—and meeting Karina—his feelings had changed. Karina loved Valentine's Day and she was one of the coolest people Robert had ever met, so how bad could it really be?

The kids found seats at the back of the auditorium, far from their classmates.

"Well, I don't care if you like it or not," Karina

14

continued. "I got you both presents, anyway." She whistled for Robert's pets, a two-headed rat named Pip and Squeak. They wriggled out of his backpack carrying two chocolate hearts wrapped in red foil. "One for each of you."

The rats crawled onto the armrest, passing out the gifts and happily chattering their teeth.

"Thanks," Robert said. "How did you get these?"

"Second-floor vending machine," she said. "Pip and Squeak fished them out for me."

Glenn studied his candy and discovered the rats had already taken a huge bite from it. He unwrapped the foil and ate the rest of the chocolate, anyway. "Isht preddy goot," he said, chewing through the caramel center. "Thanks."

Robert and Glenn were the only ones who knew that Karina had been dead for thirty years and that her spirit was confined to the property of Lovecraft Middle School. She may have looked and acted like a regular seventh-grade girl, but in truth she couldn't hold a pencil or even turn on a computer. That was why she did all of her holiday shopping from school vending machines, with a little assistance from a two-headed rat.

Karina looked pointedly to Robert, as if she were expecting a gift in return. Fortunately for him, the houselights dimmed just in time.

"The show's starting," he said.

High above the stage, a giant cardboard Cupid descended from the rafters; it was dressed in a diaper and holding a bow and arrow. A handful of students applauded, but Glenn just moaned. "Let the torture begin."

"Shhhh," Karina said

He pulled on his hood and slumped in his chair. "Wake me when it's over."

The boys and girls chorus walked on stage singing "Can You Feel the Love Tonight?" from *The Lion King*, and their soaring voices drowned out Glenn's complaints. Karina leaned forward in her chair, enchanted by the performance. After thirty years of confinement in Tillinghast Mansion, she enjoyed any chance to be a regular kid again. She was delighted by all of the everyday things that Robert took for granted: surprise fire drills, the smell of freshly sharpened pencils, and especially school assemblies.

Pip and Squeak were enjoying the concert as much as Karina, maybe even more. They sat perched on Robert's shoulder, swaying back and forth, dancing to the music.

Suddenly, Glenn sat up straight in his chair.

"I thought you were napping," Robert said.

He pointed at the stage. "Look what they're wearing!"

Robert was confused. The members of the chorus were dressed in shiny red robes. "What's the big deal?"

"They're the same robes from the mansion! The cloaks worn by Tillinghast's servants!"

Karina blinked. "Oh my gosh. He's right."

"So what?" Robert asked.

"If we got some," Glenn continued, growing excited, "I bet we could explore the whole mansion without getting caught. We could disguise ourselves as servants. Maybe we'd find a way to close the gates once and for all!"

"Maybe," Robert said, but Glenn was already standing up and gathering his things. "Where are you going?"

"To the Music Room."

"Right now?"

"We'll never have a better chance," Glenn said. "Everyone's here watching the show!"

"I'm not going anywhere," Karina said, crossing her arms over her chest. "The concert just started."

Pip and Squeak leapt onto her armrest and nodded their heads. They weren't going anywhere, either.

Glenn turned to Robert. "What's more important?" he asked. "A stupid Valentine's Day concert or saving the world from an army of ancient monsters?"

When Glenn put the question that way, Robert felt as though he had no choice. "I guess saving the world."

"I'll save your seats," Karina offered. "Have fun."

Robert and Glenn slipped out the back door and went straight to the Music Room, a large rehearsal space cluttered with folding chairs and music stands. Perched on a shelf were white marble busts of Mozart and Beethoven. Apart from the two famous composers, the boys had the whole space to themselves.

Glenn opened a door marked WARDROBE and they entered a cramped, narrow passage. It was flanked by theater costumes, marching band uniforms, and—all the way in the back—a rack of abnormally sized chorus robes. Glenn flipped through the hangers, checking the tags. "They've got extra-small or extra-extra-large," he said. "Which do you want?"

Robert glanced around anxiously. He worried that one of the music teachers would catch them red-handed. "I don't care," he whispered. "You pick."

Glenn grabbed a 2XL, pulled it over his head, and fit his arms through the sleeves.

"Why are you putting it on?" Robert asked.

"We're taking a test-drive," Glenn said. "Look."

He parted the robes, creating a gap in the middle of the clothes rack. Hidden behind the gowns was a small whirling vortex: a new gate into Tillinghast Mansion.

"No way," Robert said. "We can't ditch Karina at the concert. She's waiting for us."

"We'll be back in five minutes," Glenn promised. "I only want to take a quick peek. To see where we end up. If there's any trouble—"

"There's *always* trouble. Every time we cross over, something tries to eat us."

"If we see anything dangerous, we'll come right back."

Robert didn't share any of Glenn's curiosity. He had no desire to return to Tillinghast Mansion. The house was a giant labyrinth of cobwebbed corridors, twisting stairs, and mysterious passages. All of its doors were identical and unmarked, so it was impossible for visitors to find their way, and strange creatures lurked around every corner. Robert would have been much happier listening to love songs from *The Lion King*.

But Glenn insisted on going, and Robert couldn't let his best friend cross over alone. There was no telling what might happen if he did.

"Five minutes," he said. "Not a second more."

Robert pulled a robe over his head and wiggled his arms through the sleeves. The fabric hung past his fingertips, but it would have to do.

Glenn sat down on a box and unlaced his boots. "Don't forget to take off your shoes," he said. "All the servants walk barefoot."

"Right." He pulled off his sneakers and socks and tucked them with his backpack under a shelf.

"See you in the mansion," Glenn said, and then he

ducked between the robes and tumbled into the vortex.

Robert took one last look around the closet, nagged by a sense that he was making a terrible mistake.

Then he stepped into the gate, anyway.

CHAPTER

THREE

And suddenly he was outside.

In the cold.

Very high off the ground.

If there hadn't been such a strong wind blowing at his back, Robert would have tumbled right off the ledge. He had no idea what was going on. He looked down and nearly swooned.

Glenn reached over and steadied him. "Don't look down!" he said, shouting over the blustery winds. "We need to find a way into the mansion!"

"We're not outside the mansion," Robert said. In his brief heart-stopping glimpse down below, he had seen a softball field and a 400-meter athletic track.

"We're outside the school!"

It didn't make sense. Gates in Lovecraft Middle School were supposed to lead to Tillinghast Mansion. They weren't supposed to lead to other places in Lovecraft Middle School.

And yet this one had. The remains of the vortex lingered in the air above their heads, just beyond reach. Returning through the gate was not an option.

Glenn insisted on walking to the balcony, but nothing could convince Robert to move, not even the arrival of snow. The flakes accumulated quickly on his head and shoulders, but he didn't dare reach to wipe them away. He was frozen with fear—and soon he would be frozen, period.

"I want you to tell my mother everything," Robert said.

"What do you mean?" Glenn asked.

"If I fall. I don't want her to think I went crazy and jumped off the roof. You need to tell her the truth."

A few weeks earlier, Robert's mother had begun

24

working as head nurse of Lovecraft Middle School. She had no idea it was the sort of place where students would find themselves mysteriously transported to a narrow ledge four stories above the ground. She thought it was just a regular middle school.

"Also, there's an envelope in my backpack," Robert continued. "I need you to give it to Karina."

"What kind of envelope?"

"It's red. Sort of card shaped. You can't miss it."

"A red card-shaped envelope?" Glenn might have had a reputation as Dunwich's biggest and meanest bully, but he wasn't stupid. "You got Karina a valentine?"

"It's just Garfield. We're not dating or anything."

"Garfield the cat? From the comics?"

"He was her favorite character back in 1982, when she was still, you know," Robert explained. "She talks about Garfield all the time."

"Why didn't you give it to her before?" Glenn asked.

"I haven't had a chance."

That wasn't exactly true. Robert had had plenty of chances, but he'd spent all morning trying to work up the nerve. Even though it was just a Garfield card with a silly caption, he still felt nervous giving a valentine to a girl.

"You should've given it to her at the concert," Glenn said. "After she gave us the chocolates."

"I know."

"That was the perfect chance."

"*I know.* Will you please just give it to her?"

"Fine," Glenn said, "but I'm going to read it."

"You're not allowed to."

"Why not? I like Garfield. He's funny. Besides, if you fall off this ledge, everyone in school's going to read it. They'll publish it in the school newspaper under your photo. It'll be like your last will and testament."

Robert hadn't anticipated this, but he knew Glenn was right. Three months ago, when Nurse Mandis and Howard Mergler drowned in a lake that mysteriously sprang from the soccer field, the school mourned their deaths with all kinds of tributes and memorials. Everyone would want to read Robert's last words.

"But it's cool," Glenn said. "I mean, I'm sure you

26

didn't write anything embarrassing, right?"

Actually, Robert had. Instead of signing the card with "from," he had written the word "love"—but he would rather die than admit this to Glenn or anyone else.

Suddenly, it seemed very important that he deliver the card himself.

"I'll try walking one more time," he decided.

Robert inched toward the corner of the building, taking the tiniest of baby steps. When that didn't kill him, he took another.

"All right," he admitted, "this isn't so bad."

"You've gone three inches," Glenn said.

The ledge was already covered with a thin layer of snow, but Robert managed to take bigger steps without slipping. The wind was blowing at his back, pressing him against the stone wall, almost propping him up. Robert told himself it was just like walking on a sidewalk curb—if there was such a thing as a forty-foot-tall sidewalk curb.

They soon arrived at the corner. The ledge wrapped all the way around the building—it was a square corner—but Robert would have to step away from the wall to make the turn.

"Be careful," Glenn said. "I bet the crosswinds are pretty rough."

"What are crosswinds?" Robert asked.

"All the wind on this side of the building? It's coming from the north," Glenn explained. "And all the wind around the corner is from the east. But when you make that turn? And step out on the corner? You'll have two winds blowing at the same time. In different directions. Crosswinds."

Robert shook his head. "And meanwhile you're failing three classes. How do you know this stuff?"

"My grandfather was a sailor." Glenn shrugged. "All he ever talked about was wind."

"So what should I do?"

"Be quick. And don't look down."

Robert knew that if he tried to think of a better strategy, he'd never move. He stepped out onto the corner and the crosswinds snapped at the bottom of his robe, shaking him like a ragdoll. He pivoted on his left heel, spinning around, his other leg swinging out in midair.

To Glenn, it looked like his best friend had done a ballerina spin right off the side of the building.

"Robert!" he shouted. He leaned over, peering around the corner, relieved to find his friend clinging to the wall, practically kissing the stone. "Are you all right?"

"I'm fi-fi-fine," Robert said. "Give me your hand."

He helped Glenn navigate the corner, and then the boys continued side-stepping along the ledge. On this side of the building, the snowdrifts were accumulating more quickly; some were already two and three inches high. The boys were close enough to see the balcony. It extended from the side of the building, a ten-by-ten platform surrounded by an iron railing.

Robert quickened his steps. He was no longer thinking about falling. He was thinking about hot chocolate in the cafeteria and the warm socks he'd left in the Music Room. He was thinking about the knitted hat and gloves on the top shelf of his locker. He was thinking he might wear them for the rest of the day, even in class, even if he looked ridiculous.

As he hurried along, looking forward to all these things, he didn't notice the cracked rain gutter near the roofline, or the thin vein of ice trailing down the wall. He didn't even notice the janitor in the hooded parka, carrying a snow shovel, until the man stepped to the edge of the balcony and hollered, "What are you idiots doing?"

Robert was so startled, he slipped off the ledge.

FOUR

The janitor grabbed Robert's wrist, catching him just in time and hoisting him over the railing. Robert landed hard, scraping his palms on coarse concrete, but he didn't care. He was simply glad to be back on solid ground. If the janitor hadn't been yelling his head off, Robert could have curled up and slept like a baby.

"Are you two out of your minds?" He yanked Glenn by the arm and pulled him over the railing, too. "Do you have any idea how lucky you are? If I hadn't come up here to gather the snow shovels, you'd both be splotches on the sidewalk!"

The janitor's name was Martin McGinnis, but every kid in Lovecraft Middle School knew him as

"Maniac" Mac. He was a tall, shambling mess of a man, with a weathered face, chopped brown hair, and a drooping mustache. He kept to himself and never chatted with students, which resulted in all kids of rumors: Mac was an ex-Marine who gunned down hundreds of men in the Gulf War. Mac had spent two years in a hospital for the insane. Mac lived in a junkyard in a broken-down ice cream truck.

"Could we please go inside?" Glenn asked. "We're freezing."

"Of course you're freezing! There's a huge blizzard on the way and you morons are running around barefoot! Where are your shoes?"

"Blizzard?" Robert asked. Earlier that morning, he had listened to the radio, and there had been no mention of snow.

"A nor'easter! They're predicting thirty-six inches! Maybe more. And guess who has to shovel it?" Mac's voice was enraged, as if he somehow blamed Robert and Glenn for causing the entire storm. He stomped across the balcony and flung open the door. "Now get inside."

There were plenty of beautiful rooms in Lovecraft Middle School, but the space they entered may have been the finest. Comfortable sofas and armchairs were arranged throughout the room. Soft classical music played on a hidden stereo system. Beautiful paintings hung on the walls. Glenn looked around in awe. "What is this place?" he whispered.

"Teachers' Lounge," Mac explained. Robert moved to sit down but Mac shook his head. "We've got no business in here. Keep moving."

He led the boys out of the lounge, down a hallway, and through a door marked DO NOT ENTER. After climbing a short staircase, they surfaced in a cramped rooftop shed. In the center was a rickety wooden table littered with cookie crumbs and playing cards. Mac gestured dramatically at the dirty windows and their drab view of the roof. "Welcome to the Janitor's Lounge. Make yourselves comfortable."

Robert and Glenn fell into chairs, exhausted, while Mac rummaged through his shelves. Finally he unearthed a large canvas drop cloth spattered with paint. "Here's a blanket," he said, tossing it to the boys. Then he filled two paper cups with thick black coffee. "Drink this."

"We don't like coffee," Glenn said.

"And I don't like rescuing wise guys who think it's funny to walk on a snow-covered ledge. But here I am."

Robert was happy just to cradle the warm cup in

his hands, to hold the steaming liquid beneath his chin. With every passing moment indoors, his face felt a little less numb.

Mac took his shovel outside and pushed it across the rooftop. Robert realized he was trying to clear snow off the solar panels, but the snow was falling faster than Mac could shovel it away. After clearing six of the panels, he looked back and saw the first three were already covered again.

Mac gave up and returned inside, throwing down the shovel and stomping his boots.

"What's going to happen to the power?" Robert asked.

"That's my problem, not yours," Mac said. "Let me see your feet."

Robert held them out. Already, the pink was fading from his extremities; Mac flicked his finger against a big toe and Robert cried out in surprise.

"Did that hurt?" he asked.

"Yes!"

"Good. It means they won't have to amputate it. Do

you knuckleheads realize how close you came to dying?"

Closer than you know, Robert thought.

"Now, I am going to give you one chance to explain yourselves," Mac said. "And I want the truth."

Robert didn't know what to say. He knew Mac wouldn't believe the truth. He figured the fastest way to get out of the janitor's lounge—and get back to the concert—would be to make up a believable story.

"Glenn dared me to do it," he said. "He said he'd give me ten bucks if I put on a chorus robe and walked around the whole ledge barefoot."

Mac sipped his coffee but said nothing.

"Yeah, totally," Glenn said, doing his best to act the part. "Boy, that was such a dumb bet! What were we thinking? We could have been killed! For ten lousy dollars!"

Outside, the wind whipped against the windows, shaking the shed, threatening to rip it right off the roof.

"So, uh, can we go now?" Glenn asked.

"I don't believe you," Mac said. "I think you boys are lying to me."

"It's the truth," Robert insisted.

Mac shrugged. "Is that so, Robert? Fine. Let's go tell this story to the school nurse."

It never occurred to Robert that Maniac Mac knew his name, let alone his mother.

"You know my mom?"

"Sure, she's a very nice lady. Patched me up last month after I gashed my hand on a broken window." Mac held up his palm, revealing a hideous purple scab. "Let's see what Mrs. Arthur thinks of your story."

He marched the boys out of the roof shed and down to the first floor. Robert felt like a prisoner walking along Death Row. Lying to a janitor had been hard enough. There was no way his mother would ever believe him.

Just before they reached the nurse's office, Mac's cell phone chirped. He ordered the boys to halt and answered it. Robert couldn't tell what the conversation was about, but it didn't seem to make Mac any happier. "I understand," he said. "I'm on my way." Then he clicked off the phone and turned to the boys.

"On second thought, I'm going to deal with you clowns later. I need to go."

"What's happening?" Robert asked.

"They're evacuating the school. State of emergency. They want everyone out of the building in the next hour."

CHAPTER

FIVE

———

Mac told the boys to grab their socks and sneakers and then report to the cafeteria, where their classmates were waiting to be evacuated. Instead, Robert and Glenn went straight to the library. Whenever anything strange happened at Lovecraft Middle School, they always headed to the school librarian, Ms. Claudine Lavinia, for good advice.

She was their most trusted ally—the only adult who knew the truth about the school. She was also Crawford Tillinghast's sister and had been working with Robert and Glenn to foil her brother's plans.

Most mornings, they could find her at the library's circulation desk. Today, an unknown woman was standing in her place. She had a long narrow face, and her dark hair was pulled back in a bun. She saw the boys and frowned. "Library's closed," she explained.

"Where's Ms. Lavinia?" Glenn asked.

The woman straightened. "She's fallen ill. My name is Miss Carcasse and I'll be teaching all of the library lessons until Ms. Lavinia returns."

Robert had been at Lovecraft Middle School long enough to recognize all the usual substitute teachers, and he'd never seen this person before. A funny smell tickled his nose, and he realized it was Miss Carcasse's perfume.

Glenn crossed his arms over his chest. "It's freezing in here," he said. "Is the air conditioning on?"

"I'm quite comfortable," she said. "Many libraries can be drafty, but in our profession one gets used to it."

Robert had never felt a draft in Lovecraft Middle School before. There were no leaks or cracks or rattling windows. The building was just six months old, practically brand new.

"Something's wrong," he said, stepping inside for a closer look.

Miss Carcasse hopped out of her chair, blocking his way. She moved with a curious limp, as if one of her legs was longer than the other, or perhaps her knees didn't bend properly. Up close, her perfume was overpowering. It smelled like a nauseating blend of blooming roses and burning hair.

Robert looked past her to the computer lab and saw a fine layer of snow atop one of the keyboards. More flurries were blowing in through a wide-open window. "That machine's getting ruined!"

"Whoops," Miss Carcasse said, walking calmly to the window and pulling it closed. "Looks like someone was careless." She didn't seem concerned that the computer was likely destroyed. "Now it's time for you boys to leave. You can go to the cafeteria with everyone else, or I'll send you straight to the principal's orifice."

The boys stared back at her

"You mean the principal's *office*?" Glenn asked.

Miss Carcasse frowned. "That's what I said."

The boys chose the cafeteria instead.

"Something's up," Glenn muttered.

"Oh, yeah," Robert agreed. "Something's definitely up."

CHAPTER SIX

When the boys arrived in the cafeteria, Robert's mother was standing on a small platform at the front of the room, addressing the students with a microphone. "I need everyone to pay attention," she was saying. "This is a very dangerous storm. We already have three inches of snow on the ground . . ." The rest of her sentence was lost beneath a round of cheers and applause.

Robert wasn't thrilled when his mother started working at Lovecraft Middle School, but he had to admit she seemed a lot happier. She loved helping children, and she often bragged that Lovecraft was one of the top-ranked schools in the region. She seemed completely oblivious to the strange things happening there day in and day out.

"I want you all to look out these windows," Mrs. Arthur said. Normally, the cafeteria offered a panoramic view of the front lawns and the long winding driveway that led toward town. Today, it was like peering through a giant snow globe. "These are whiteout conditions. When you step outside, you won't see more than five or six feet in any direction. It's extremely disorienting and very dangerous. That's why *no students can leave the school today without adult supervision.*"

There was a lot of eye-rolling and a couple of kids groaned, but Mrs. Arthur said that she meant business. "If your parents are already here, you're dismissed. The rest of you will leave by bus. We'll begin loading now by homeroom. Will everyone in Room 115 please line up by the door?" She clapped her hands. "Come on, everybody, on your feet!"

Other teachers were helping guide the students into orderly lines. When Mrs. Arthur recognized her son, she came hurrying over.

"Where have you been?" she exclaimed. "I've been looking everywhere."

"Sorry," he shrugged. "I was—"

"Listen to me, Robert. Don't get on the bus. I've got our car in the parking lot, and as soon as everyone's safe, I'll drive us home." She turned to Glenn, who ate dinner at their house nearly every night and was practically part of the family. "You, too, Glenn. Come with us."

"No, thanks," Glenn said. "If there's a bus leaving now, I'm getting on it. The sooner I get out of here, the better."

Glenn grabbed his backpack and got in line with the other kids in his homeroom. Mrs. Arthur returned to the microphone and called out more directions. Robert took a seat in the back of the cafeteria and looked out the windows.

Six yellow school buses were idling in the driveway; Maniac Mac was out in the snow, shoveling furiously, carving a path so that kids could get onboard.

Across the driveway, the teachers were rushing out of the faculty parking lot, their cars fish-tailing over the snow, the engines revving helplessly. A crossing guard with a STOP sign ran shouting from one vehicle to the next, trying to bring order to chaos.

Karina dropped into a chair beside Robert. "Some Valentine's Day, huh?"

"Sorry we missed the concert." He explained how he and Glenn had ended up trapped on a ledge four stories above the ground, and Karina just nodded matter-of-factly, as if these sorts of things happened all the time.

"I'm glad you didn't fall," she said. "You'd really hate being a ghost."

"Do you still have Pip and Squeak?"

"They're napping in the gym. Do you mind if I watch them for a few days?"

"Sure," Robert said. "They love it when you babysit."

Karina once confessed that Saturdays and Sundays were her least favorite days of the week because she was trapped in the school all by herself. With a nor'easter on the way, she could be facing a week or more of solitary confinement. Having Pip and Squeak would take her mind off the loneliness.

Mrs. Arthur kept calling homeroom numbers, and more and more students were exiting the cafeteria. Soon only a few dozen kids were left.

"I should leave," Karina said, "before your mom tries to stick me on a bus."

"Where will you go?"

"I'll just hide in the locker room until everyone's gone. See you in a couple days, I guess."

Robert thought of the Garfield valentine in his backpack and decided this was as good a moment as he was likely to get.

"Hang on."

He reached into his backpack, looking for the red envelope, but it was no longer there. He emptied all his textbooks but still couldn't find it. Robert was certain he had it at the concert—yet somehow the card had mysteriously vanished.

"What are you looking for?" Karina asked.

Suddenly Robert felt foolish and empty-handed. He removed a raisin granola bar from his knapsack and placed it on the windowsill.

"For Pip and Squeak," he explained. "In case they get hungry."

CHAPTER

SEVEN

Long after the other teachers had all left for home, Mrs. Arthur was still hurrying around the cafeteria, barking orders until the last of the students had boarded buses. And even then, she wasn't ready to leave. She walked around turning off lights.

"We need to go," Robert said.

"Lights are expensive," Mrs. Arthur said. "When you have to pay your own electric bill, you'll know what I mean. Help me find the switches."

Robert was looking for a way to turn off the kitchen lights when Maniac Mac appeared in the doorway, glaring at him. "What are *you* still doing here?"

"I'm sorry," Robert stammered. "I was—"

Mac turned to Mrs. Arthur. "You need to leave," he said. "The driveway's turning into a ski slope. It's a mess. Pretty soon it won't be safe to drive."

"I'm just getting the lights," Mrs. Arthur said.

"*I'll* get the lights," Mac said. "It's my job. Take your son and go before it's too late."

Robert was relieved. In all the excitement over the blizzard, Mac seemed to have forgotten to tell his mother about the ledge.

"What about you?" Mrs. Arthur asked.

"I've got my truck. I'll be right behind you," Mac promised. "Now please, go home. Drive safe."

Robert and his mother gathered their things and left the building through the front entrance. Even though Mac had just shoveled the walkway, it was already covered with a fresh layer of powder. He hadn't exaggerated: The snow was coming down harder than ever.

Despite the blizzard, Robert and his mother both stopped to admire the strange surreal beauty of the landscape—the rolling lawns draped in white, the tall trees frosted with snow. All the buses were gone. All the students were gone. All except one shivering boy standing beneath a lamppost and looking up and down the driveway. Lionel Quincy.

Mrs. Arthur hurried over to him. "What are you doing here?" she exclaimed. "Why aren't you on a bus?"

He crossed his arms over his chest. "I don't like buses."

"How do you expect to get home?"

Lionel held up his cell phone. "I left my father a voicemail. I've asked him to send a driver."

Lionel was one of Robert's least favorite classmates. He boasted to anyone who would listen that his father was the inventor of PerfectPrice, a website worth millions of dollars. Lionel had recently moved to Dunwich, Massachusetts, and he was constantly bragging about all of his rich friends back in New York City.

Mrs. Arthur frowned. "Let me explain something, Lionel. This is a state of emergency. No chauffeur is going to slog through this mess. You were supposed to get on a bus."

"Fine," Lionel shrugged. "Call me a new bus and

I'll get on it, all right?"

"There are no more buses! You missed the last one!" She shook her head, exasperated. "I'll have to drive you home myself. Where do you live?"

"Wait, what?" Robert asked.

"Up in the Heights," Lionel said.

The houses in the Heights were among the nicest in town—giant mansions built on tall cliffs overlooking the ocean. But to get there, you had to ascend a series of absurdly steep hills.

"Our car will never make it," Robert said.

"We have to try," Mrs. Arthur said. "Everyone else is gone. I can't leave him waiting in the middle of the blizzard."

Together they trudged across the driveway, leaning into the wind, faces down. Robert sank up to his ankles in the snow. The faculty parking lot was empty except for Mac's pickup truck and his mother's tiny two-door Honda; cocooned beneath a white blanket, the vehicles looked like giant marshmallows. Robert brushed the side windows with his gloves while Mrs.

Arthur cleared off the windshields with an ice scraper. Lionel stood by, his hands shoved in pockets, waiting for them to finish.

"That's good enough," Mrs. Arthur said. "Get in."

Lionel climbed into the backseat and wrinkled his nose. "It smells funny."

"You'll get used to it," Mrs. Arthur said. "We had an accident back in October." The accident being that Robert left his window open on the day of a sunshower, and the upholstery had been plagued with mold and mildew ever since. Robert was glad his mother didn't go into detail.

Lionel lifted his shirtfront over his mouth and nose. "Can you crack the windows or something?"

"We're driving through a blizzard," Mrs. Arthur reminded him. "I'm not opening the windows."

She turned the key in the ignition, and the engine growled and sputtered without turning over. This was typical; on really cold days, their car needed a lot of coaxing before it would start.

Lionel leaned forward from the backseat. "What's

the matter?"

"Nothing's the matter," Robert said.

Mrs. Arthur tried again, and the engine made a desperate groaning wheeze. Snow was spotting up the windshield, slowly dimming the interior of the car.

"Something's the matter," Lionel said. "You put a key in a car, it's supposed to turn on."

"It'll turn on," Mrs. Arthur said.

She tried again: no luck.

"Give it a minute," Robert said. "Let it rest."

Fat snowflakes pelted the windshield, plugging the gaps like pieces of a jigsaw puzzle falling into place.

Lionel brought out his cell phone and punched in a number. "I'll try my dad again," he said. "I'm sure he can send someone." He held the phone to his ear, waited a moment, and then frowned. It didn't seem to be working.

"One more try," Mrs. Arthur said.

She turned the key again and this time, incredibly, the engine purred to life, as if it had been functioning normally all along.

"Buckle up," she said.

Robert and Lionel fastened their seat belts and Mrs. Arthur flipped on the wipers, slashing a view through the windshield. She pressed on the gas pedal but the tires spun helplessly over the ice. For a moment, it seemed like they might not be going anywhere.

But then the wheels found traction and the Honda surged forward, hurtling out of the parking lot and cutting fresh tracks down the middle of the driveway.

It was a narrow quarter-mile road that stretched past the school, the athletic arena, and the tennis courts. Mrs. Arthur leaned forward in her seat, both hands clutching the wheel, puttering along at fifteen miles an hour.

"This is going to take *forever*," Lionel moaned.

Mrs. Arthur ignored him. Snow pelted the windshield and the wiper blades couldn't push it away fast enough. She turned the steering wheel, following the curve of the driveway as it passed through a dense grove of pine trees. The snow had already risen above the curb; it was impossible to see where the road ended and the forest began.

"You need to go faster," Robert said.

"It's too icy."

"We won't make it up the hill."

The school driveway ended with a steep climb to Phillips Avenue, the main highway into town. Mrs. Arthur pressed on the gas, increasing their speed to thirty.

"Faster," Robert said. "We need momentum."

"It's too dangerous," Mrs. Arthur insisted. "I can't see."

"We're going to get stuck."

"That's better than hitting a tree."

But Mrs. Arthur increased her speed anyway, accelerating all the way to forty miles an hour. The car refused to travel in a straight line; it swerved left and right, sliding all over the ice. The wipers were tossing snow across the windshield; there was no chance of seeing the hill in this mess, but Robert kept waiting to *feel* it, knowing that gravity would slow their ascent.

And then, all at once, they were upon it:

A blue minivan, stalled in the middle of the road.

"Mom!" Robert shouted.

Mrs. Arthur cut the steering wheel and hit the brakes, but it was too late. Robert put out his hands, bracing himself for impact, and the vehicles collided with a sickening crunch.

CHAPTER

EIGHT

The next time Robert opened his eyes, he had snow on his face and chest. He appeared to be outside, but somehow he was still wearing a seat belt. His lap was filled with thousands of tiny glittering diamonds. Robert reached down and cupped them with his gloved hands.

I'm rich, he thought.

"Are you okay?" Mrs. Arthur was saying. "Robert, honey, can you hear me? Are you all right?"

And just like waking from a dream, Robert was back in the Honda. He realized he was merely *looking* outside; the passenger-side window had shattered, and the diamonds in his lap were actually tiny pebbles of tempered glass.

"I'm fine," he said. "I'm all right."

Mrs. Arthur turned around to face Lionel. "How about you? Is everything okay?"

"Give me a break," he said. "Nothing about this situation is okay."

Mrs. Arthur hurried out of the car. Robert reached to open his door but it wouldn't budge. He shook the broken glass from his lap, then climbed over the gearshift and exited through his mother's door.

Robert had walked along this road every day for six months—but seeing it now, shrouded in snow, it looked wholly unfamiliar. It may as well have been Alaska.

Mrs. Arthur was already helping the other driver out of her vehicle. She was a tall thin woman who walked with a limp. Robert recognized her as Miss Carcasse, the substitute teacher who chased him and Glenn from the library.

"I'm so sorry," she was saying. "This is all my fault."

Robert's mother put an arm around her. "You're in

shock. I want you to relax and take a deep breath. Do you have a coat?"

All Miss Carcasse wore was a blue turtleneck and slacks—no hat, no scarf, no gloves. "I'm afraid I forgot it," she said. "I was so anxious to get home, I guess I wasn't thinking."

Mrs. Arthur gave her car keys to Robert. "Go get the picnic blanket. We need to keep her warm."

Robert puzzled over Miss Carcasse's remarks as he unlocked the trunk of the car Who leaves school in the middle of a blizzard and forgets to put on a jacket?

He gave the blanket to his mother and she draped it around Miss Carcasse's shoulders. Up close, even in the middle of a blizzard, he could still smell her awful perfume. She was explaining that she had tried and failed to get her minivan up the hill. "Three times I tried, but it's just too icy. And now we're stuck here. What are we going to do?"

The cars weren't going anywhere without the help of a tow truck. Already they were disappearing beneath a layer of white powder, as if the surrounding landscape was trying to swallow them up.

"I'll hike into town," Robert volunteered. "I'll find a grown-up and bring back help."

"No way," his mother said. "Too dangerous."

"We can't stay here. What are we going to do?"

The wind whipped past them, a slow and steady howling through the trees. Robert turned toward town—or where he thought town might be. He couldn't see more than ten feet ahead. The wind was blowing so hard, it was difficult to keep his eyes open. The howling grew louder and louder, and Robert realized it wasn't wind at all.

It was an engine.

"Car!" he exclaimed.

His mother just stared at him.

"Someone's coming! Get out of the road!"

Then the wind subsided and Mrs. Arthur heard the engine, too. It was revving up, accelerating as it approached the base of the hill. She took Miss Carcasse by the arm and hurried her to safety. Robert was following them until he remembered that Lionel Quincy was still inside the Honda. The boy was lying across the backseat with his eyes closed, listening to headphones.

"Lionel!" Robert opened the door, reached in the backseat, and yanked off the headphones. "Someone's coming!"

"Is it my driver?"

"No, not your driver. Get out of the car!"

Headlights pierced through the snowfall, glinting in the rearview mirror, and at once Lionel understood the danger: low visibility, two wrecked cars, and no time to stop. He grabbed his phone and leapt from the vehicle just as a black pickup truck emerged from the blizzard.

The driver turned the wheels and hit the brakes but momentum carried the truck forward; it smashed into the Honda, pinning it against the minivan with a squeal of metal and the loud *bang!* of a punctured tire. The impact shook the snow from the surrounding trees.

"Oh, no," Mrs. Arthur gasped.

The door to the truck swung open and Maniac Mac hopped out, wide eyed and panicked. "Is everyone all right?" he asked. "Is anyone hurt?"

"We're all fine," Robert said.

Mac ran over to check the disabled vehicles. Only when he confirmed they were empty did he stop to take a breath.

"I'm so sorry," he said. "I didn't see you until it was too late."

"We know," Mrs. Arthur said. "The same thing happened to us."

Mac inspected the damage on his vehicle. The truck slouched forward on a flattened front tire. The headlights were shattered. The hood and grill were crumpled inward like an accordion. Robert thought the undamaged parts of the truck didn't look much better. It was a real clunker, at least thirty years old and covered with dents and scratches. And yet Mac seemed devastated by the accident.

"I think I should walk into town," Robert told him. "It's our only option."

Mac shook his head. "Don't be stupid. You'll never make it in this weather."

"Exactly," Mrs. Arthur said. "We're staying together."

Lionel was trying his cell phone again, pacing in circles with the device raised above his head, searching for a signal. When he didn't find one, he threw down the phone and stomped on the screen with the heel of his boot. "Cheap piece of garbage!"

"Relax, it's just the storm," Mac said. "It's interfering with the cell towers. Your phone's working just fine."

Not anymore, Robert thought. The cell phone lay scattered in pieces on the road. Robert could think of dozens of occasions when he'd asked his mother for his own cell phone, but her answer was always no, not until he saved enough money to pay for it himself.

"Mac, what about the school?" Mrs. Arthur asked. "Don't you have the keys?"

He nodded. "That's a good idea. There's a land line in the principal's office," he said. "We can call for help and stay there until someone comes."

They each gathered their belongings from the vehicles and began the long march back to the building.

Miss Carcasse could barely move in the deep snow; Mac wrapped an arm around her waist, helping her along. "Careful!" she said. "Not so rough!"

"All right, take it easy," he said.

She stumbled forward and something dropped out of her side. Robert stopped to collect it and realized it was a greasy purple earthworm, six or seven inches long. He left it alone and hurried to catch up with the group.

"I'm sorry about your truck," Mrs. Arthur said.

"Trucks can be replaced," Mac said. "We're lucky none of us were killed."

"There are fates worse than death," Miss Carcasse said.

"What does that mean?" Robert asked.

"She's in shock," Mrs. Arthur whispered to Mac. "She's been a little confused since the accident."

"What I mean is that humans have always feared dying," Miss Carcasse continued. "But there are worse things in this universe. Forces beyond our knowledge or comprehension."

"Like what?" Robert asked.

"Please," his mother interrupted. "Let's stay focused on the positive."

They emerged from the grove of pine trees and the blizzard surrounded them; it looked more like a sandstorm than any snowfall Robert had ever seen. Fortunately Mac's tires had left a convenient trail through the oblivion. After several minutes of walking, an outline of the school slowly came into view.

"We'll use the main entrance," Mac said. "It should be straight ahead."

The building looked dark and foreboding in the gloom of the blizzard. All the lights were off except for a single classroom on the second floor. Karina Ortiz sat within the window frame, staring out at the falling snow.

Mrs. Arthur saw her and gasped.

"I forgot someone!"

CHAPTER

NINE

Karina's performance was so convincing, Robert had to remind himself she was only *pretending* to be a frightened student left behind in a snowstorm. She even managed to fake some tears. "I d-d-don't know what happened," she blubbered. "I was reading a book in the library and I guess I fell asleep. When I woke up, everyone was gone. And all the lights were off. I was so scared. I thought I would be trapped here all by my-self—"

"There, there," Mrs. Arthur said, reaching to comfort her. Karina backed away just in time. "Have we met before? Did you come for your vision and hearing test last month?"

All Lovecraft Middle School students had their eyes and ears examined by the school nurse once a year. All the living students, that is.

"We met at the Halloween dance," Karina reminded her. "The night Robert was elected student council president. I'm Karina Ortiz."

"I knew you looked familiar," Mrs. Arthur said.

They were all gathered in the lobby just inside the main entrance. No one had removed hats or gloves or scarves; they were all still thoroughly chilled. Miss Carcasse stood near the doors to the outside, watching the snow and occasionally squinting, as if she were looking for something.

"Let's go to the principal's office," Mac said.

He used his keys to open the door, and the others followed. It was a large room with four desks for assistants and smaller, separate offices for the principal and her associates. Mrs. Arthur picked up a phone and dialed 9-1-1 while Mac turned on a television and searched for a weather report. Miss Carcasse went over to the window, opened the blinds, and continued watching the snow.

Karina stood next to Robert. "What's the deal with her?"

"My mother thinks she's in shock," Robert said, "but if you ask me, she was acting weird before the accident." He told her all about Miss Carcasse's strange behavior in the library.

"She's holding something," Karina whispered. "Look at her hands. What's she doing?"

It was a small gold object that resembled a pocket watch—but instead of a traditional clock face, this device had a dial that was numbered 0 to 100. Robert moved closer for a better look and saw the needle was pointing to 18. Miss Carcasse noticed him looking and put the device in her pocket.

"Over here, everybody!" Mac called.

He had found a weather report on TV. The meteorologist stood before an animated map of the Massachusetts coast. Most of the beaches were clear, but the area over Dunwich was covered with snowflakes. "We've never seen anything like this," she was saying.

"It's a very small storm, just ten miles wide, and appears to be stalled over the village of Dunwich. Residents can expect anywhere from forty to even fifty inches of snow before tomorrow morning. I repeat, we've never seen *anything* like this."

Karina turned to Robert. "I don't like the sound of that."

He knew exactly what she was thinking: it was too weird to be a coincidence. If Crawford Tillinghast had the ability to engineer an entire dimension, he certainly could engineer a little snow.

But why?

Why create an enormous snowstorm over the school?

"It's gotta be global warming," Mac decided. "It's causing all kinds of crazy weather. Hurricanes, tsunamis, and now this. When are those stupid politicians going to wake up and realize it?"

On the other side of the office, Mrs. Arthur began shouting into the telephone. "Hello, can you hear me? Are you still there?"

"What's wrong?" Robert asked.

"Disconnected," she said, hanging up. "I guess the wires went down. I did manage to reach the police, though. They know we're here, and they're going to send a rescue team."

"Fantastic," Mac said.

"There's just one problem," she added. "They can't get here until the storm clears. Tomorrow morning at the earliest."

It took a moment for the news to sink in.

"Are you kidding me?" Lionel exclaimed.

"None of us are happy about this," Mrs. Arthur said.

"I'm not staying here all night. You need to talk to Chief Russell. He's friends with my father."

"I *did* talk to Chief Russell."

"He knows I'm here?"

"He knows we're here. He knows we're okay."

"But we're not okay," Lionel said. "What are we supposed to eat? Where will we sleep? On the floors?"

Karina rolled her eyes. "You'll survive."

If Miss Carcasse was upset by the news, she didn't show it. She continued staring out the window and occasionally moved her lips, as if whispering to herself.

"Let's be grateful for the things we *do* have," Mrs. Arthur said. "A warm building, basic first aid and supplies, and plenty of food in the cafeteria. There's even TV and Internet. All things considered, I'd say we're pretty lucky."

"Exactly right," Mac said. "There are plenty of people in worse shape right now. People without shelter or water or heat, people who don't even have—"

And then, all at once, the TV went dark.

And every light in the office flickered out.

CHAPTER

TEN

Mrs. Arthur looked to Mac. "Power failure?"

"Impossible," he said. "The school has a huge generator. If the power goes out, it should turn on automatically."

Lionel put his hands on his hips. "So now we *don't* have Internet? We don't even have lights?"

"Relax," Mac said. "If the generator's broken, I'll fix it. Everybody stay here until I get back." He turned to Robert. "But you come with me. I might need someone to give me a hand."

They left the office and set off down the hallway. Even though the power was out, the corridors weren't completely dark; every so many feet, illuminated EXIT signs emitted a faint red glow.

"How come those are still working?" Robert asked.

"They have backup batteries," Mac explained. "Same as the smoke detectors. But they won't be much help if I can't fix the generator."

"I thought you said you could?"

"I said that so people would calm down," Mac explained. "That substitute? Miss Carcasse? She's already acting nutty, and your pal Lionel isn't much better."

"He's not my pal."

Mac raised an eyebrow. "He's not?"

Robert shrugged. "He only hangs out with kids who live in the Heights. He's stuck-up that way."

"Well, a lot of people are," Mac said.

They stopped in front of a wide door marked FREIGHT/DELIVERIES and Mac reached for his key ring. "Look, there's something we need to get straight. This business with the ledge. You're probably wondering why I haven't told your mother."

Robert's stomach flip-flopped. Ever since the collision in the driveway, he'd been waiting for Mac to bring it up.

"She deserves to know," Mac continued. "But I've decided not to tell her until we get out of this mess. We don't need any extra tension right now. So you can stop worrying, all right?"

"Okay," Robert said. "Thanks."

Mac unlocked the door but it wouldn't budge. "Now get out of my way. Give me some room." He threw his shoulder against the door; it opened an inch and snow flurries sprayed through the gap. Tall drifts were accumulating outside the building, barricading the exits.

"Is there another way to the generator?" Robert asked.

"Not if we want to get there before dark," Mac said.

He tried again—he threw all of his weight against the door—but again it barely budged. The gap had widened to three inches, not nearly enough for Mac to squeeze through.

"Let me try," Robert said.

He turned sideways, wriggled through the opening, and climbed out onto a loading dock. Almost immediately, he was up to his knees in the tall drifts—and more snow was falling fast, piling up against the walls of the building. Robert was glad he'd kept his gloves on. He reached down and swatted snow away from the door, digging with his hands like a dog, until there was just enough of an opening for Mac to push his way out.

Then they both stared out at the parking lot. It was like looking across a vast arctic tundra; penguins and polar bears would have seemed right at home.

"Storm's getting worse," Robert said.

"Oh, yeah?" Mac asked. "Are you a weatherman or something?"

"It just looks different. Like it's getting stronger."

"Well, we didn't come to admire the pretty scenery. Let's get moving."

They hopped off the loading dock and sank knee-deep in the massive drifts. Robert felt like they were leaving the safety of a beach and wading out into a wild and turbulent sea. He worried he wouldn't be able to keep up, but Mac slowed his pace so Robert wouldn't be left behind.

"Don't you need tools or something?" Robert asked, shouting to be heard over the wind.

"Tools won't help me," Mac shouted back. "I don't know how to fix a generator."

"Then what are we doing out here?"

"I'm hoping it has a power button. Maybe someone forgot to turn it on." He reached out and grabbed Robert's shoulder, pulling him backward. "Careful now, look where you're walking."

At their feet was a large hole about the width of a basketball. It seemed to be the opening of a tunnel that burrowed underneath the snow. Robert peered inside but couldn't see very far; it was like looking down the dark drain of a sink.

"Not so close," Mac said. "If you fall down that hole, I'm not going to fish you out."

On the far side of the hole was the generator—a large rectangular box about the size of a railroad car, with slatted vents and long, raking claw marks over the front. The side panel had been peeled back like the lid

of a tin can. Frayed bands of wires dangled out of the generator, as if someone or something had bitten clean through them.

Mac whistled through his teeth.

"What happened?" Robert asked.

"I have no idea," he said. "But I think we better get back inside."

CHAPTER
ELEVEN

Mac didn't tell the others about the strange scratches on the generator; he decided they were the work of a bear, and he didn't want to cause further panic. He simply explained that the generator was beyond repair.

Lionel scowled. "You said you could fix it."

"You're welcome to fix it yourself," Mac said.

"I'm not sticking around," Lionel assured him. "As soon as my dad gets my voicemails, he's going to freak out. He'll charter a dozen snowplows and get me out of here." He called to Miss Carcasse, who was still perched in front of the window. "Tell me when you see them coming, okay?"

Miss Carcasse didn't answer. She was studying the view so carefully, she might have been counting the snowflakes.

"Why don't you lie down?" Mrs. Arthur asked. "Come over to the sofa and take a rest."

Miss Carcasse turned and smiled. "I'm fine right here," she said. "It's like watching a beautiful winter wonderland." She checked the mysterious gold object again, then returned to the window.

"We've got less than two hours until it's pitch dark," Mac announced. "Our top priority should be finding a light source." He unsnapped a large chest marked with a red cross. "This emergency kit has two flashlights and a lantern, but they won't get us very far."

No one could think of an alternative, however, until Robert remembered his second-period social studies class. "We're making beeswax candles with Mrs. Zelley," he said. "It's a project on life in colonial America. She's got dozens of them."

"Perfect." Mac turned to Lionel. "Go to Mrs. Zelley's classroom and bring back all the candles you can carry."

"Why me?" Lionel asked. "Why can't Robert do it?"

"Because he and Karina are going to fix the heat. It's already way too cold in this building." Mac passed the lantern to Robert; it was a simple battery-operated lamp, the kind you might take on a camping trip. "I want you guys to walk around and close the doors to every classroom. That will insulate the core of the school."

"Sure, that's easy," Robert said.

"Meanwhile, I'll poke around the school store," Mac said. "See if they have anything we can use."

"And I'll go to the cafeteria," Mrs. Arthur volunteered. "I can look in the kitchen and start figuring out meals. Miss Carcasse can help me."

"Excellent," Mac said. "Let's all meet there in half an hour."

Once they'd all gone their separate ways, Robert turned on the lantern, its tiny incandescent bulb flickering to life. It wasn't very bright—the batteries seemed to be dying—so Robert switched it back off.

For now, there was still enough daylight for him and Karina to navigate the hallways. They set off toward the east end of the school. Robert closed the classroom doors while Karina skipped along beside him.

"What are you so excited about?" he asked.

She grinned. "Do you know how long it's been since I've gone to a slumber party? This is going to be awesome!"

"If we survive," he said. Robert told her about the strange scratches on the generator and the mysterious tunnel descending into the earth. "Something's out there in the snow. Something very powerful. And I think Miss Carcasse is looking for it."

"She's one of Tillinghast's creatures?"

"She has to be," Robert said. "She's acting weird, she's walking weird, she even smells weird. That awful perfume? It's probably masking her true scent."

Karina nodded. "This day keeps getting stranger and stranger."

"And it's not over yet," Robert said. "Look who's coming."

Pip and Squeak were scampering down the hall-way, hurrying to meet them. The rats ran straight up Robert's leg and perched on his shoulder, chattering wildly and gesturing with their tiny arms.

"Calm down," Robert told them. "What's wrong?"

Come come see see now quick—

Over the past few months, Robert had become quite good at "hearing" his pets' thoughts—but because the rats usually communicated simultaneously, their words sometimes echoed in his mind. Often, the messages were hopelessly jumbled.

"One at a time," Robert said. "Pip first. What is it?"

Follow. Hurry. Bring light.

The rats didn't wait to see if Robert understood. They simply raced down the hall, and he and Karina had no choice but to hurry after them. They rounded a corner and ran straight through a snowdrift—a large mound of slush piled high in the center of the hall. Robert's legs went out from under him. He fell on his back, landing hard on the slick wet floor.

"Are you all right?" Karina asked. She reached out

to help, and her hand passed through his elbow, chilling the joint like a blast of ice water.

Robert rubbed the back of his head. All around him, the air was filled with snowflakes, a miniature micro-blizzard right in the middle of the hallway. "I think I'm seeing things," he said. "It looks like it's snowing indoors."

"It *is* snowing indoors," she told him. Robert sat up and snowflakes settled on his hair and shoulders, but they passed through Karina as if she wasn't even there. "It's coming from the chemistry lab."

They passed through the open doorway and it felt like they were stepping outside. The Periodic Table of Elements was covered with frost. The lab counters, chairs, and sinks were buried beneath inches of snow. And all the large windows were shattered. Shards of glass were piled at the edge of the classroom, as if something had crashed through from the outside.

Robert turned to his pets. "Did the storm do this?"

No, no, this was the Old Ores.

The words sounded familiar to Robert; over the

past few months, he had heard Professor Goyle, the Price sisters, and Howard Mergler speak with awe and admiration of the great Old Ones. But who were they?

Pip and Squeak led him and Karina to the windowsill and crawled outside, leading them to the edge of a large round hole. It looked just like the passage Robert had seen near the generator—except this one was bigger, as if an even larger creature had come through it.

Robert knelt beside his pets and lowered his voice to a whisper, in case whatever built the tunnel might still be lurking nearby. "Did the Old Ones come out of this tunnel? Are they inside the school?"

Not yet. Not ready yet. Too warm.

Pip and Squeak scampered inside the tunnel and looked back at Robert and Karina, expecting them to follow.

"No way," Robert said. "Not a chance. The last time we crawled into a tunnel, I ended up in a Dumpster full of larvae."

He was referring to an incident three months ago,

when Pip and Squeak had vanished inside the school's ventilation system, and Robert, Glenn, and Karina had to crawl into the ducts to retrieve them.

"You don't have to worry about bugs," Karina assured him. "They can't survive in the cold. Whatever made this tunnel is definitely a warm-blooded mammal."

"And big enough to break all these windows," Robert said. "I don't need to go chasing after it."

Pip and Squeak plunged deeper into the passage, their long pink tail trailing behind them. Robert peered inside the opening and choked on the odor. It smelled like the guinea pig cage in the library.

"Can you see anything?" Karina asked.

Robert switched on the lantern and held it inside the tunnel. Bits of dirt and debris were embedded in the packed snow, as if something unclean had recently passed through.

"Let's take a quick look," Karina said. "If we see anything dangerous, we'll turn around and come right back."

"That's what Glenn said this morning," Robert

told her. "That's how I ended up on a ledge forty feet above the ground."

Still, he got down on his hands and knees and crawled in, anyway. Robert quickly realized that the passage wasn't simply traveling beneath the snow; it was descending into the ground, through a tunnel that someone or something had burrowed into the earth. As they crawled along, the passage expanded, until it was tall enough for Robert and Karina to stand.

CHAPTER
TWELVE

"What is this place?" Karina whispered. Her voice echoed throughout the tunnel. Clusters of icicles hung from the ceiling like stalactites. Ahead of them, icy stone steps descended into darkness.

"I have no idea," Robert replied. He had never heard of an underground cavern anywhere in the village of Dunwich. And yet this space seemed like it had existed for centuries. Robert snapped a small icicle from the ceiling and tossed it down the stairs; it disappeared into the gaping black void without making a sound.

"You really want to go down there?" Karina asked.

"No," Robert said, "but if Pip and Squeak think

it's important, we should."

He moved cautiously from one step to the next, descending lower into the abyss, arms outstretched to keep his balance. His worn-out sneakers had terrible traction, and he knew one false move would send him tumbling all the way down.

"Glenn is going to be sorry he went home," Karina said.

Robert laughed. "Right now Glenn is sitting in a warm room watching television. Getting on that bus is the smartest thing he ever did."

"Well, I'm glad you stuck around," she said. "This is a lot more fun than babysitting your rats."

Robert stepped on something that felt like a bundle of sticks. "Watch out!"

At their feet was a human skeleton, sprawled across several of the steps, as if the person had died while attempting to climb out.

"Yikes," Karina said. "What happened to that guy?"

A small leather satchel hung from the skeleton's shoulder. Robert reached into a pocket and pulled out

a faded identification card. DR. WILLIAM DYER, it read. PRO-
FESSOR OF GEOLOGY, MISKATONIC UNIVERSITY EXPLORERS' SOCI-
ETY. FEBRUARY 1936.

Robert showed the card to Pip and Squeak. "This
is what you wanted me to see?"

No, no, keep going—

"What'd they say?" Karina asked.

"They keep saying it's fine," Robert said. "But after
meeting Professor Dyer, I'm finding it hard to believe
them."

They continued their descent, venturing lower and
lower into the earth, and the unpleasant smell grew
ever more pungent. Eventually the steps ended and the
passage widened into an enormous cavern, much too
big for the lantern to fully illuminate. Pip and Squeak
ran up Robert's chest and plunged into the hood of his
jacket, as if they had no intention of walking any far-
ther on their own.

"What's wrong?" Robert asked.

Old Ones! Coming!

Robert squinted into the shadows but didn't see

anything.

"On the floor," Karina said. "Look."

A tiny puff of fur wobbled toward them. It wasn't much larger than a pom-pom. Robert lowered the lantern and the little puffball shrieked, as if the light hurt its eyes.

"Whoa, sorry," he said, dimming the lantern until there was just enough of a glow to find the creature in the dark. "Why, it's just a baby! Come here, little fella. Don't be afraid."

Yes, be afraid, be very afraid—

Robert shook his head. "There's no way this little puffball broke all those windows."

"Of course not," Karina agreed, leaning down for a closer look. "They're just jealous because he's cute! He's like an itty-bitty hamster!"

The puffball crouched low to the ground, shivering on the ice, seemingly terrified. Robert couldn't help himself. He reached out to pet it and the creature's mouth sprang open, quick as a mousetrap, revealing two wide rows of fangs. Robert yanked away his fingers just in time.

"Some itty-bitty hamster!" he exclaimed. Now the puffball was snarling at him, enraged at missing an opportunity for a free lunch. Robert turned up the glow of the lantern, and the furball frantically hopped away.

"Uh-oh," Karina said.

Robert raised the lantern and realized the creature wasn't alone. There were dozens—no, hundreds—more waiting in the shadows, and most were much bigger. The Old Ones resembled short flat-footed trolls with stumpy arms and legs; their round bodies were covered with matted and tangled fur. As the light reached them, they shrieked and shielded their big black eyes.

"Listen to me very carefully," Karina said. "Whatever you do, *do not drop that lantern.*"

"Right," he said. "Let's go."

Together they slowly backed up the staircase. Robert waved the lantern back and forth, casting its glow around the cavern to keep the Old Ones at bay. The creatures followed them from a distance, snapping

and snarling as if such threats might frighten Robert into dropping the lamp and falling down the steps. Clearly, the trick had worked at least once before, on Dr. William Dyer of Miskatonic University. Robert stepped backward over the professor's remains, careful not to trip on the bones.

"There must be three hundred of those things," Karina whispered. "No wonder Pip and Squeak wanted us to see them."

The Old Ones moved like ants swarming from a nest; they shared a group mentality and advanced in a pack. One of the creatures grabbed Dr. Dyer's femur and flung it up the stairs; the bone missed Robert by inches.

"Look out!" Karina said.

The others joined in the assault, flinging ribs and vertebrae, screeching taunts and pelting Robert with bones. Dr. Dyer's skull hit the side of the lantern, nearly shattering it. Robert kicked the skull back at them, toppling the closest creatures like bowling pins.

When he and Karina finally surfaced in the middle of the still-raging blizzard, the Old Ones remained huddled beneath the earth. Karina looked up at the fading sky.

"It's the daylight," she said. "They must be waiting for the sun to go down."

"And then what?"

Karina looked at the shattered windows. "Then I'm guessing they want to join our slumber party."

Returning to the chemistry lab, Robert and Karina began looking for something that might contain the Old Ones inside the tunnel. Robert considered covering the hole with some kind of obstruction, but he guessed nothing would stop the creatures except light.

"What if we left the lantern?" Karina asked.

He shook his head. "The batteries are dying."

They searched the lab for batteries, and when that didn't turn up anything, they switched to looking for an alternative light source. All Robert could find was a red butane lighter, the sort of wand used to light candles and barbecue grills. He clicked it on, and a pale blue flame emerged from the tip.

"Careful," Karina said.

"Fire would hold them back," Robert said. "If it burned all night, they would never come inside this room."

"Fire could also burn down the school," Karina reminded him. "This is a chemistry lab, remember?"

"Exactly!" he exclaimed.

He remembered that every workstation was equipped with a valve for propane gas. By attaching a Bunsen burner to the valve, students could have a small flame-powered torch for heating beakers and test tubes. Robert assembled a burner to demonstrate, and it produced a steady, tall, yellow flame that illuminated one corner of the classroom.

"We'll light three more," Robert decided. "One in each corner. Pip and Squeak can stay here and stand guard. Make sure the flames are under control." He turned to his pets. "Will you do that for me? Will you come get me if the fires go out?"

Yes okay yes sure.

Karina looked under the countertop, inspecting the large propane tank that fueled the entire lab. "You think there's enough gas to keep the lights burning all night?"

"We better hope so," Robert said. "If the Old Ones get inside this building, we're never getting out."

CHAPTER

THIRTEEN

It was nearly dark when Robert and Karina finished setting up the Bunsen burners and returned to the cafeteria. Beeswax candles were arranged around the tables, casting the room in a moody, ethereal glow. It felt more like a medieval cathedral than a place where kids feasted on hot dogs and tater tots.

Lionel was standing on a table near the windows, holding a second cell phone above his head. This new phone was housed in a lime green case; it was slightly bigger than the one he'd smashed outside.

"You have two cell phones?" Karina asked.

Lionel shrugged. "It's the easiest way to back up your data. Everyone in my family has two phones."

Robert was flabbergasted. Most of the twelve-year-olds he knew would have been thrilled just to have one.

Outside the building, Mac was flailing against the squall, struggling to post sheets of cardboard on the windows. Miss Carcasse watched him struggling and chuckled, as if she found the whole display amusing.

"What's he doing out there?" Robert asked.

"Hanging up signs," Miss Carcasse explained. "Alerting rescue workers to our location. Just in case they show up while we're sleeping." Mac slipped on an ice patch, falling, and Miss Carcasse chuckled again. It didn't seem very funny to Robert.

He realized she was holding the gold trinket again—only now, the dial had dropped to 14.

"What is that thing?" he asked.

"Why do you ask so many questions?"

"I'm just curious."

"It's a thermometer," she explained. "It measures temperatures in Celsius, so the numbers are lower than you're used to."

"Why do you have a thermometer?"

"Because I like to be aware of my natural surroundings," she explained. "That's the problem with young people and all of your electronic gadgets. You're completely ignorant of the natural world."

She turned back to the window and absently twirled a length of hair with her finger. Robert watched as she twisted the strand tighter and tighter until the hair popped loose from her skull, leaving a small hole. A pale pink worm wriggled out, twitching this way and that, like it was sniffing the air.

"My goodness, excuse me," Miss Carcasse said, pressing one hand to the side of her head and limping toward the restroom.

"Was that a worm?" Karina whispered.

"She's full of them," Robert said. He explained how he had seen another worm drop out of Miss Carcasse while they were trudging up the driveway.

"Now we know why she wears so much perfume," Karina said. "She must be rotten on the inside. Some kind of reanimated corpse, like a zombie, disguised with fresh hair and skin."

This would also explain Miss Carcasse's strange walk and bizarre behavior—but Robert didn't understand why she'd left school when the blizzard started. "If she's from Tillinghast Mansion, why did she try to leave? Why was she trying to get up the driveway?"

"Maybe her brain's rotten, too," Karina said. "Maybe she can't think straight."

They went into the kitchen to look for Robert's mother. They found her standing over a boiling pot, stirring its contents with a long wooden spoon.

"I hope you guys are hungry," she said.

Real hungry, Robert thought. *With all this talk about rotting brains, I'm practically starving.*

"What's for dinner?" he asked.

"The gas still works, so I put together a soup," she said. "Can you kids set the table?"

She gestured to a stack of napkins, bowls, and plastic sporks. Karina hesitated, so Robert swept in. "I'll get it," he said.

He carried everything out to the cafeteria and set

a table for six near the windows. Lionel watched him working but didn't offer to help.

"Any luck with the signal?" Robert asked.

Lionel shook his head. "I wish I could get an Internet connection. If I got a signal, I'd just go on PerfectPrice and hire someone to pick us up."

"In this weather?" Robert asked. "I doubt it."

"You can pay anyone to do anything," Lionel insisted. "That's the point of PerfectPrice. You can hire any person for any job if you're willing to pay the perfect price." He sounded like he was quoting a television commercial.

"And that works?" Robert asked. "People do it?"

"Sure, it works! That's why my dad's in the September issue of *Fortune* magazine. That's why he's the 87th Most Powerful Titan in the Tech Industry." Lionel checked his cell phone and frowned. "But I guess we're stuck here until the cell phones start working."

Robert felt like he ought to warn Lionel about the frozen chemistry lab and the Old Ones. Instead, he just said, "I think we'll be safer tonight if we all stick together. Stay with the group. Don't go wandering off by yourself."

"Right," Lionel said. "Because it's really cool hanging out with a janitor and a psycho substitute and your mom. No offense."

Mac came inside, stamping his boots and shaking the snow from his clothes. "There must be two feet out there already," he said. "That's practically six inches an hour. It has to be some kind of record."

Mrs. Arthur emerged from the kitchen as Miss Carcasse returned from the restroom. "You're just in time for dinner," she announced. "Let's eat."

They all sat down at the table. In addition to the soup, there were all kinds of cafeteria foods: apples, bananas, snack bags of baby carrots, peanut butter crackers, chocolate milk for the kids, and hot tea for the adults.

"This is a feast!" Mac exclaimed. "My compliments to the chef."

"Well, happy Valentine's Day," Mrs. Arthur said. "I tried to make the most of a bad situation."

Robert tasted his soup. "It's good."

"Good? Young man, this is delicious," Mac said. "This is the best thing I've tasted in weeks."

Mrs. Arthur blushed. "It's just odds and ends."

Lionel took a sip, frowned, and set down his spoon. "Is there any pizza?"

Mac grunted. "I'd like to see you cook pizza on a stovetop."

Miss Carcasse tried lifting her plastic spork but kept dropping it, as if she'd never handled a utensil before. Finally, she pushed her soup away. "I'm afraid my nerves are too jumbled. I don't think I could keep it down."

Robert and Karina exchanged skeptical glances. They knew that all of Tillinghast's creatures hated the taste of cooked food. They preferred the taste of raw meat or, better yet, meat that was still breathing.

Mrs. Arthur turned to Karina. "How about you? Are you feeling better? You haven't touched your dinner."

Karina stared helplessly at her spork, but of course she couldn't touch it. She couldn't even place her napkin in her lap.

"It looks delicious," she said, "but I can't . . . I just . . . I'm sorry."

"What's wrong?" Mrs. Arthur asked.

Karina fumbled for a convincing excuse. She looked past Mrs. Arthur to the windows, as if she might find an answer in the snowstorm.

And then she screamed.

Outside the building, a man looked back at her.

He was short, only five feet tall, and completely enshrouded in snow. His face was a void with three small holes: two eyes and a mouth.

He pounded icy fists on the glass.

And then collapsed.

Mac was already on his feet. "Come on," he told Robert. "I'll need your help."

They ran out into the storm. The figure lay immobile at the base of the windows. Mac reached behind his head and peeled back what appeared to be a black ski mask. Underneath was the familiar face of Glenn Torkells.

"Let's get him inside," Mac shouted, reaching under Glenn's shoulders and lifting him off the ground. "Grab his feet."

Together they carried Glenn into the cafeteria and set him on an empty dining table. Mrs. Arthur sprang into action, calling out for supplies. "Somebody boil water. And bring some candles over here. We need blankets, lots of blankets. And scissors. Something to cut off these clothes. They're frozen solid."

As everyone scattered to collect the items, Robert stood over the body of his best friend. Glenn's eyes opened. His body shook uncontrollably.

"What are you doing here?" Robert asked. "I thought you were taking the bus home."

"I her-her-heard you were stuck here," Glenn explained. "The police chief was on the T-T-TV news."

"So you walked back here in the blizzard? Are you nuts?"

"I had to warn you."

"Warn me?" Robert asked. "About what?"

"The chief said your mother called him from the

109

school. He said six people were trapped. There had been a car accident."

"That's right," Robert said. "Miss Carcasse was stalled at the bottom of the driveway, and my mother smashed right into her."

Glenn shook his head. Even though they had brought him indoors, his chills seemed to be getting worse. Like they were overtaking his entire body.

"I saw Miss Carcasse when we were le-le-leaving," Glenn said. "Ou-ou-out the window of the bus. There was no accident."

"I saw it," Robert insisted. "There was definitely an accident."

Glenn shook his head more frantically. "She did it on purpose," he explained. "She's trapped you here *for a reason*."

Then he stopped shivering and closed his eyes.

CHAPTER

FOURTEEN

Mrs. Arthur spent the next hour caring for Glenn, cutting off his frozen clothes with kitchen scissors, and then dressing him in the warmest garments that Robert and Karina could find: a wool sweater from the school lost-and-found box, trousers from a marching band uniform, and long sport socks from the gymnasium.

"Is he going to be all right?" Robert asked.

"He's lucky he's alive," Mrs. Arthur said. "I've seen twelve-year-olds do a lot of stupid things, but walking through a blizzard takes the cake."

"Does he need a doctor?"

"His pulse is low, but it's getting stronger. His

temperature's almost back to normal. Hopefully he just needs rest, because I've done everything we can do for him."

They had moved to the basketball gym for the evening, and Mac dragged out tumbling mats for everyone to sleep on. Boys on one side of the court, girls on the other.

Miss Carcasse seemed confused. "We're all sleeping together? In the same room?"

"It's safer this way," Mac said. "In case there's an emergency."

Robert thought of the Old Ones lurking just outside the chemistry lab and the propane burners keeping them at bay. "I agree with Mac," he said. "I'll feel a lot safer if we're all in the same room. With the doors locked."

"Don't be ridiculous!" Miss Carcasse said. "What if a rescue crew arrives? How do you expect them to find us? These doors should be unlocked at all times."

"I've left signs outside," Mac reminded her. "If anyone comes, they'll know exactly where to find us."

Miss Carcasse looked around in frustration, but it seemed everyone in the group agreed with Mac. "Suit yourselves," she shrugged. "In the end, your actions have no meaningful consequences. Your fates were decided long ago."

She lay down on her mat without any blankets or even a jacket, then crossed her arms over her chest and closed her eyes. It wasn't even seven-thirty, yet Miss Carcasse immediately went to sleep.

"She's just tired," Mrs. Arthur decided. "It's been a long day."

"A very long day," Mac agreed.

He placed the lantern on the half-court line, directly between the two groups. Mac had replaced the batteries with new ones, but still the lantern wasn't much brighter than a candle. In the vast gymnasium, it looked like a tiny campfire on a sprawling open plain.

Robert and his mother paced in circles to stay warm. The temperature inside was dropping with every passing minute, and they were all wearing extra sweatshirts borrowed from the school store. Mac went out to the vending machines to collect some junk food, but they found most of it was frozen solid. Lionel bit into an Oreo and nearly chipped his tooth.

"That's it," he decided. "I'm going to bed."

Mac offered him a choice of blankets: heavy black drapes from the school theater, colorful patchwork quilts from the art room, heavy-duty plastic trash bags, terrycloth towels from the swimming pool, and more paint-spattered drop cloths from the janitor's lounge.

"Use as many layers as you can stand," Mac advised him. "It's important that you stay warm."

Lionel didn't seem pleased with any of the choices, but he took a trash bag and a drop cloth and stomped off toward his mat without saying goodnight to anyone.

Mrs. Arthur checked on Glenn one last time—he was doing fine, she said—and announced she was going to sleep as well. "It's too dark and cold to do anything else," Mac agreed. "I'll lock the doors."

Robert and Karina weren't ready to sleep just yet, so they climbed to the tops of the bleachers, where their conversation wouldn't disturb the others. They were so far from the lantern, they were practically in the dark.

"Some slumber party, huh?" Robert asked.

"It's definitely a night to remember," Karina said.

He pointed down to Miss Carcasse, sleeping with both hands folded in her lap, like a corpse on display at a funeral. "Do you think it's safe to go to bed? Will she try anything?"

"She can barely walk," Karina reminded him. "Heck, she can't even lift a fork. By the time we wake up, I bet she's nothing but a pile of worms."

Robert knew Karina was right. As long as the doors stayed locked and the lantern stayed on, they had nothing to worry about. "I can't believe I'm going to spend the night in Lovecraft Middle School," he said. "What would you be doing if we weren't here?"

"Oh, the usual stuff. Floating up and down the hallways. Moaning and wailing and rattling my chains.

It's a very exciting life, being a ghost."

"I'm serious," Robert said.

"You want the truth? I know this has been a tough day. Between the blizzard and the car accident and the ice cavern and now poor Glenn. But having you and your mom around like this? Sitting down at a table for a homemade dinner? And camping out in the gymnasium? It's been a real blast. I'll be sorry tomorrow when you have to leave."

Robert realized this was the opportunity he'd been waiting for that morning—the perfect chance to give Karina the Valentine's Day card. But since it had vanished from his backpack, all he had to give her was a shrug. And this made him angry, because he felt she deserved better.

"I'll be sorry tomorrow when you can't come with us," he said. "It's not fair that you're stuck here."

"At least tomorrow's still a long way off," she said.

They sat on the bleachers for a long time afterward, not saying anything else, and finally they walked down to their mats. Robert wriggled into a plastic trash bag, pulled a theater drape over his body, and used his backpack as a pillow. It was probably the most uncomfortable "bed" he'd ever crawled into, and yet he fell asleep almost instantly.

CHAPTER

FIFTEEN

Robert awoke to bristles tickling his face, as if someone was dabbing his cheek with a paintbrush. He opened his eyes and realized Pip and Squeak were sitting on his neck, nudging him with their noses.

It was the middle of the night. He pushed off the drape and sat up. The clock above the scoreboard read 3:30. Lionel, Mac, and Glenn were still asleep. The rats were pacing in circles at his feet, frenzied with excitement.

"How did you get in here?" he whispered.

Come, come, light, light, light.

Robert wriggled out of the trash bag and stood up. Somehow the door to the gymnasium was wide open, even though he was certain he'd seen Mac lock it.

"Is it the propane? Are the lights off?"

No worse much worse. It's the lady.

Robert glanced at the three mats on the other side of the gymnasium. He recognized his mother and Karina, but Miss Carcasse's mat was empty.

Come come come, the rats called, already scampering toward the door. Robert grabbed a flashlight and hesitated. He wished he could bring help, but Glenn needed his rest and he didn't dare wake Karina, not with his mother sleeping so close. He would have to go alone.

Pip and Squeak led him out of the gymnasium and through the east wing of the school. Robert switched on his flashlight and saw the lockers were covered in frost; somehow the temperature inside the school had fallen to below freezing. He could see the breath coming out of his own mouth.

All the doors he'd closed earlier had been reopened; Robert peered into a classroom and saw that its windows were open. All the classrooms had their windows wide open.

As they approached the chemistry lab, Robert heard a voice echoing through the darkness. "*Antra gnomorum! Veni, veni, veni! Expergisciimini!*" The language sounded ancient and incomprehensible, but Robert knew he recognized the speaker.

He stopped in the doorway. All the Bunsen burners were extinguished; the laboratory was dark. The drifts were even deeper now, knee-high in places. Miss Carcasse stood before the shattered windows, calling out into the night.

"*Veni, veni, veni! Coventus Gnomorum!*"

One of the furry white creatures climbed through the broken window and hopped down to the laboratory floor, waddling toward Miss Carcasse on its short stubby legs. Another creature, even bigger than the first, followed behind. This one carried Professor Dyer's tibia over its shoulder, brandishing the bone like a club.

Robert flipped on the flashlight and the Old Ones shrieked, shielding their eyes and toppling backward.

"Turn that off!" Miss Carcasse yelled.

He no longer recognized her. She limped toward him, shambling forward, her pursed lips twisted into an evil, demented grin. Her skin was pale and punctuated with throbbing blue veins. Worms wriggled from her ears and fell to the floor. A long string of black ooze drained from her nostrils.

"Don't let my appearance trouble you," she explained. "This vessel has never fit me properly. But now that the *gnomorum* have risen, I no longer need it!" She held up her hands and out popped ten sharp fingernails, like a cat springing its claws.

She pounced toward Robert and he darted away, with Pip and Squeak racing alongside him. He realized too late that his best hope was to return to the gymnasium, but he was already running in the wrong direction. Miss Carcasse was chasing after him, cackling madly. The corridor ended at the Music Room; Robert hurried inside, closed the door, and locked it.

Keys, keys, she has keys, Pip and Squeak warned.

Of course. Miss Carcasse had stolen Mac's keys to unlock the doors to the gymnasium. And now she would unlock the door to the Music Room, too. Already, he could hear her fumbling with the lock, trying the keys one by one.

"The Old Ones have been dormant for centuries!" she called out. "They need sustenance, Robert! They're hungry! That's why Master sent me out in the blizzard—to trap live meat for the Old Ones to feast upon! You and your companions will make an excellent meal!"

Robert aimed his flashlight around the room. The marble busts of Mozart and Beethoven stared down with their stern expressions. The room had no windows and no other exits.

They were trapped.

"Find someplace to hide," he told Pip and Squeak. "Don't worry about me. Just get out of here."

They all fumbled around in the dark, colliding with folding chairs and toppling music stands. Pip and Squeak wriggled inside the bell of a trombone. Robert tripped over a tangle of rope and fell to the floor. He realized the rope was attached to a giant cardboard Cupid, the same cheesy prop that had descended from the rafters during the Valentine's Day concert.

It gave Robert an idea.

He knelt down to examine the rope. It was only an inch thick—not ideal, but hopefully it was strong enough. A few knots were tied in its length, and Robert tied off some more. Then he ran into the wardrobe and hid among the chorus robes. He left the flashlight on so it would be easy for Miss Carcasse to find him.

A minute later, she arrived in the wardrobe, along with some two dozen snarling and snapping creatures. The Old Ones were ravenously hungry . . . and Robert's flashlight was the only thing keeping them at a distance.

"Turn off the light," Miss Carcasse told him. "I promise death will be instantaneous. They'll strip the meat from your bones in minutes. And what an honorable way to die! At last, your wasted human flesh can fulfill a higher purpose! *Ave, ave Gnomorum! Ave Gnomorum!*"

More and more creatures were pushing and shoving their way into the wardrobe, climbing on top of one another, filling the space with their awful pungent odor.

Miss Carcasse stepped forward with the same weird demonic grin, as if it were frozen in place.

"Turn off the light," she repeated. "Surrender to us!"

Robert knew he had to time his next move exactly. He allowed Miss Carcasse to get closer—close enough that he could smell her hideous perfume. Then he switched off the light and leaned backward, falling into the rack of chorus robes.

By the time Miss Carcasse pounced, Robert was already outside, four stories above the school and falling fast. This time, the high ledge surrounding Lovecraft Middle School was buried beneath icy snowdrifts, leaving no place for him to land.

But it didn't matter. His body hung suspended in midair, spinning in the wind. One end of the knotted rope was woven through his belt loops in a sort of harness; the other end was back in the wardrobe, anchored to a railing.

Miss Carcasse didn't have time to realize how she'd

been tricked. She followed Robert through the vortex and shrieked as she tumbled past him, reaching out with her clawed fingers. "No!" she shrieked. "*Valete Gnomorummmmmmmm . . .*"

Robert looked away before she hit the icy ground below.

Now for the hard part, Robert thought. He shoved the flashlight in his back pocket and then grabbed the knots in the rope, pulling himself up, hand over hand. He used the tips he'd learned in gym class: climb with your legs, not your arms. Pinch the rope with your feet. Step on the knots. It wasn't easy, but the centripetal force of the vortex helped him along, offsetting gravity, reeling him up like a fish on a line.

After surfacing in the wardrobe closet and untying the rope, Robert realized his problems were far from over. Yes, Miss Carcasse was gone—but now hundreds of Old Ones were loose in the school, and Robert could hear them wreaking havoc in the Music Room. He stepped into the chaos and turned on the flashlight. The creatures were stomping on the piano keys and pulling apart the cardboard cupid, breaking off its arms and legs, eating its limbs. Others were gnawing on the marble busts of Mozart and Beethoven, trying to chew off their faces. Still more were banging the trombone on the floor, trying to shake Pip and Squeak from their hiding place.

But on Robert's arrival they all stopped, set aside their distractions, and advanced toward him.

"Stay back!" he warned, waving his flashlight back and forth. It was like fending off a pack of wild dogs with a whiffle ball bat. The creatures kept advancing, saliva dripping from their jaws, their stumpy arms reaching toward him.

Robert kept his back to the wall, inching out of the room and into the hallway, but the entire herd followed along. He couldn't outrun them and he couldn't out-fight them. He needed light—and dawn was still several hours away.

More Old Ones were waiting in the hallway, and Robert realized he had unwittingly placed himself in the center of the pack. Now he had creatures behind him and creatures advancing toward him—but only one flashlight.

A glowing red EXIT sign alerted him to an emergency access door. Robert dreaded the idea of going into the blizzard, but he didn't have a choice. The creatures were closing in. He backed up against the door, hitting the push bar with his elbow. The lock seemed to release but the door wouldn t budge. Robert tried

again, hitting it harder, throwing his weight against it. He realized there was too much snow on the opposite side—the drifts were barricading the exit.

The Old Ones seemed to understand his predicament; their black eyes twinkled with amusement as they closed ranks, standing body to body, leaving him nowhere to run.

And then a voice cut through the darkness.

"*Sistite! Discumbere gnomorun!*"

At once, the creatures dropped to their knees, lowering their foreheads to the floor.

A tall slender man emerged from the shadows. He was dressed in a black suit and held a single candle that illuminated his face. He was old, with pale skin stretched tightly across his cheeks. "Don't mind the Old Ones. They're nasty creatures, but they'll behave if you show them who's boss."

"You're their boss?" Robert asked.

"In a manner of speaking." The old man extended his hand and smiled. "I'm Crawford Tillinghast."

CHAPTER

SIXTEEN

After hearing so much about Crawford Tillinghast for so long, Robert was surprised to see that the man was really just a thin, pale, flesh-and-blood human being—not unlike the old men who paraded through the school on Grandparents Day.

Except Tillinghast had a strength and confidence that those other old men hadn't possessed in years. When he shook Robert's hand, he held it an extra moment, squeezing harder, just to prove his point. Then he released his grip and smiled, revealing two crooked rows of yellowed teeth.

"*Aperi portam!*" he commanded, and a large gate materialized before them, spanning the full width of the hallway. The Old Ones responded with excited chirps and chattering, and Tillinghast beckoned them forward. "*Itinere gnomorum! Itinere!*"

The Old Ones broke into a stampede, pushing, shoving, and climbing over one another to reach the gate. They entered three or four at a time and immediately vanished, crossing over to the next dimension. Tillinghast watched them with pride, like a parent admiring his own children. The entire herd vanished in a matter of moments; soon all that remained of them was their awful pungent odor.

Tillinghast shouted a second incantation—"*Claude ostium!*"—and the gate dissolved, folding upon itself like an eyelid blinking shut. He sighed with tremendous satisfaction, as if a monumental task had finally been completed.

Then he set off down the hallway.

"Come," he told Robert.

Tillinghast opened the nearest door, leading them into the office of a guidance counselor. On the walls were framed photographs of waterfalls, lighthouses, and soaring eagles. Tillinghast sat in a tall leather-backed chair and placed the candle on an end table.

"Sit," he said.

Robert perched on the edge of a comfortable leather sofa. He was very tired but too scared to sit back and relax.

"Would you like something to drink? A glass of water?"

"No, thanks," Robert said.

Tillinghast removed an ancient-looking vial from his jacket and unscrewed the cap. "Well, forgive me if I indulge," he sighed. "It's been a long day."

Robert looked down at his lap. His hands were shaking. He had faced so many terrible creatures in the past six months—but none quite so frightening as the old man sitting in the guidance counselor's chair.

"You don't have to be afraid," Tillinghast said. "I just saved your life, remember?"

Robert didn't answer. He didn't know what to say.

"Don't look at your lap. Look at me. I want to have a conversation."

Robert looked up but couldn't bring himself to make eye contact. He stared past Tillinghast, over his shoulder, through a window overlooking the parking lot.

Outside, the snow had stopped falling.

"I gather you've heard some nasty things about me," Tillinghast continued. "People getting kidnapped and stuffed into urns, et cetera, et cetera, et cetera." He sighed. "The truth is, I'm a very generous person. I believe I can help you—if you're willing to discuss things."

Robert whispered the first response that came to mind: "Is the storm over?"

"Very good! Excellent question! Yes, the storm has moved out to sea. The great migration is complete. The Old Ones are safe in my mansion at last."

"Where did they come from?"

"Right here in Dunwich. Thousands of years ago, this part of the continent was teeming with them. But they moved underground when the glaciers melted." Tillinghast tipped back his head and drained the vial in a single swallow. "They're magnificent warriors but far from perfect. Two millennia of subterranean dwelling has ruined their eyesight. And they can't tolerate any climate that isn't freezing. Put them somewhere at room temperature and they shrivel up like raisins. That's why they've spent the past two thousand years in hibernation. Our planet has been too warm."

"So you manufactured a blizzard?" Robert asked.

"You're getting ahead of yourself," Tillinghast said. "First, I manufactured a climate-controlled chamber in my dimension. A place where the Old Ones can train and hopefully evolve to tolerate higher temperatures. The snowstorm was simply a means for getting them from Point A to Point B. I needed the ground to be freezing, and I needed the school to be chilled."

The longer Tillinghast spoke, the more Robert relaxed. "So, Miss Carcasse was helping you?"

"That's right. While you were all distracted by the arrival of Glenn Torkells, she walked around the school, opening windows and doors. Lowering the temperature to zero degrees Celsius." Tillinghast capped the empty vial and placed it in his pocket. "I don't appreciate the little trick you played on her, by the way. She wasn't bright, but she fulfilled her duties admirably."

"She was trying to feed me to your monsters," Robert reminded him.

Tillinghast smiled. "You're a smart boy. I've been watching you for several months. No child or adult has ever outwitted one of my associates, but somehow you've foiled six of them. Professor Goyle, Sarah and Sylvia Price, Howard Mergler, Nurse Mandis, and now Miss Carcasse. For a twelve-year-old, you're quite impressive."

"I'm just trying to stay alive," Robert said.

"I can arrange for that," Tillinghast offered. "If you're willing to help me."

"Why should I do that?"

"For starters, I've kept the Old Ones from eating your friends in the gymnasium. I'd say that deserves a thank-you. But I have an even better proposal."

He reached into his coat pocket and removed a red envelope—the valentine that Robert had purchased for Karina.

"Where did you find that?"

"Like I said, I've been watching you a long time. While you and Glenn were flailing about on the ledge, I took the liberty of going through your backpack. I hope you don't mind." He returned the card to Robert. "Has she told you she's in limbo?"

137

"I don't know what that means."

"It means that she can be made whole. She can regain her true form. She can walk and play and ride a bike; she can be a living, breathing thirteen-year-old girl who can leave this prison and never look back. All I require is a replacement. A body and soul to take her place."

"You mean me?" Robert asked.

"No, of course not. You're more useful to me here. But perhaps there's someone else."

"I don't know anyone willing to give up their body."

Tillinghast shrugged. "Perhaps this person doesn't volunteer."

"I don't understand."

"Come with me. I want to show you something."

He took the candle and led Robert across the school to the end of the east corridor, where a pair of doors led to the outside. Tillinghast tossed the ancient-looking vial at the doors and it vanished in midair, swallowed by a gate that was nearly invisible.

"I'm proposing that you lead a companion down

this hallway," Tillinghast explained, "and then that person wanders through this gate by accident."

"Accident?" Robert asked. "You mean, you want me to trick somebody?"

"There's no pain involved. We simply take the body, and the person's spirit is imprisoned. In a very large and comfortable urn."

"I don't know anyone who deserves that."

"Oh, I bet you do," Tillinghast said. "There has to be someone you don't like. Someone who's unfriendly to you. Disrespectful to your mother. Someone in this school right now."

Robert didn't have to think long. "You mean Lionel Quincy?"

Tillinghast winked. "We'd settle for him."

"No way. I couldn't."

"He thinks he's better than you. Always bragging about his money and his house in the Heights. And his amazing father. The 87th Most Powerful Titan in the Tech Industry. I say it's time to teach Lionel a lesson."

"He doesn't deserve to be imprisoned."

"Neither does Karina. But life isn't fair, Robert. Some of us have bad luck. What I'm proposing is trading one body for another. A nice girl goes free. A spoiled brat gets punished. Where's the injustice?"

Robert couldn't answer the question. He felt it was wrong, but he didn't know *why* it felt wrong. Tillinghast had managed to make a wrong choice sound right.

"It's all very simple. You'll find an excuse to lead Lionel down this hallway. The boy isn't bright; he'll believe anything. And the gate will take care of the rest. We'll be waiting on the other side to relieve him of his vessel. And Karina will be free of this place at last."

Robert shook his head. "Lionel doesn't deserve it."

"Think of it as an extended detention. A punishment. Would you agree he deserves to be punished? Doesn't Karina deserve her freedom?"

Robert looked down at the valentine. On the front of the card was a picture of Garfield with hearts exploding from his head; the caption read "I'm CRAAAZY for you!" He'd wanted to get Karina something nice for Valentine's Day, but now the card seemed silly and inconsequential. What she really wanted, more than anything else in the world, was to be free of Lovecraft Middle School once and for all.

"It feels wrong," Robert said.

"Why don't you sleep on it?" Tillinghast suggested. "Sometimes tough choices seem easier by the light of day. I'll leave the gate open just in case."

"What happens in the morning?"

"You and your friends walk out the door. Minus one, of course. Either Lionel or Karina. Whoever stays behind is up to you."

CHAPTER

SEVENTEEN

When Robert returned to the gymnasium, the rest of his group was still asleep. He tiptoed back to his tumbling mat and pulled the theater drape over his body.

Even though he was exhausted, he had trouble falling back to sleep. He couldn't stop thinking about Tillinghast's offer. *Doesn't Karina deserve her freedom? A nice girl goes free. A spoiled brat gets punished.*

Where's the injustice?

Robert tossed back and forth for a long time. Eventually he drifted off, but only for an hour or so. When he opened his eyes, the clock over the scoreboard read 6:05. Lionel and Glenn were still sleeping, but Mac was gone. Robert pulled on his shoes and went to look for him.

Out in the hallway, he heard the distant noise of a hammer striking nails. Robert followed the sound to the student woodshop. There, Mac was standing over a workbench with three long planks, joining them with a cross-brace.

"Good morning," Mac said. "You want some coffee?"

"I don't like coffee."

"Oh, that's right. I forgot."

Mac resumed working and Robert sat down to watch. He finished nailing the cross brace and then used an old-fashioned hand drill to bore two small holes into the planks. Mac fed a rope through the holes and knotted it, forming what looked like a handle.

"What are you making?" Robert asked.

"It's a sled."

"You're going sledding?"

"Your buddy Glenn is going sledding," he explained. "If he can't walk out of here this morning, I'll tow him to a hospital using this rope."

"What about the rest of us?" Robert asked.

"Come on," Mac said. "I'll show you."

He grabbed his coffee and then led Robert up to the top floor of the school. They walked through the teachers' lounge—past all the furnishings Robert had admired the day before—and then Mac opened the door to the balcony and they stepped outside.

The sky was blue, the sun was shining, and their view of Dunwich extended all the way to the ocean. Between the school and the water were shops, houses, restaurants, and churches, all buried beneath huge billows of snow. The roads were invisible; the plows had yet to clear them. Robert had never seen anything quite like it.

"Wow," he said.

Mac pointed to the forest on the edge of school property. "See that trail through the trees? It's about a mile into town. Pretty gentle downhill slope. We'll hike through there and pull Glenn on the sled."

Robert felt it was important to act as if nothing

strange had happened during the night. "What about Miss Carcasse?" he asked. "Will she fit on the sled, too?"

"Miss Carcasse is dead," Mac said. He pointed to a mound of snow at the base of the building. "When all this stuff melts, they'll find her body buried beneath that drift. But you know that already, right?"

He flashed a wicked grin, and Robert stepped away from him, half-expecting to see horns sprout from his forehead or membranous wings burst out of his back. At once, all the weird rumors surrounding Maniac Mac made sense. No wonder he hadn't mentioned the strange scratches on the generator to anyone else—he'd been working for Tillinghast all along!

But there was one thing Robert didn't understand: "If you're working for Tillinghast," he asked, "why do you care so much about getting Glenn to a hospital? Why build a sled?"

Mac laughed. "If I worked for Tillinghast, I wouldn't be mopping floors and scrubbing toilets. No, Robert, I'm trying to *stop* him. You and Glenn aren't the only ones."

Robert leaned against the railing, relieved, as Mac proceeded to share his story. He was one of the few laboratory assistants to have escaped the explosion at Tillinghast Mansion thirty years earlier. He was just sixteen years old at the time; he'd been hired to mop up in the laboratory after school for five dollars an hour. "I knew your friend Karina back then, but of course she doesn't recognize me anymore."

After the explosion, Mac spent the next three decades haunted by the awful things he had witnessed in the laboratory—and dreading the day Tillinghast would return. "I suffered from nightmares, insomnia, you name it," he explained. "I wanted to talk to someone, but who would believe me? The monsters, the alternate dimensions, it all sounded insane. People thought I was bonkers."

Over the years, Mac had tried numerous jobs—shipbuilding, carpentry, fishing, lobstering, house painting—and failed at all of them. His life was a mess. He had moved into an abandoned ice cream truck in a junkyard near the coast, where he spent his days gathering aluminum cans to redeem for nickels.

"But the day this school opened, I knew Tillinghast had found a way back, so I resolved to get here as quickly as possible. I took a job that gave me a set of keys and complete access to the building. And I've been working here ever since. I clean the desks. I shovel the snow. And I look for weaknesses in his plan."

Robert was astonished. "So you know everything?"

"I wouldn't say that. But I know how you and Glenn ended up on that ledge yesterday morning. I know why Karina can't hold a fork at dinner. I know that Miss Carcasse summoned all the Old Ones into the school." He lowered his voice. "And I know about the deal, Robert. I know what Tillinghast offered you last night."

"You do?"

"When you sneaked out of the gym, I followed you. I watched those creatures nearly devour you. And then I tracked you and Tillinghast to the guidance office. You cannot help him, Robert, do you understand me?"

"He says Lionel deserves it."

"He's tricking you. Lionel's got problems, just like everybody else. They're just different from yours."

"Some problems," Robert muttered. "It must be really tough living with a millionaire dad in the Heights."

"It's tougher than you know," Mac said. "I want to help Karina just as much as you do. But we'll have to find a different opportunity."

"The gate's still open," Robert said. "He said he'd leave it open in case I changed my mind."

"The gate will always be open. You'll spend your whole life hearing from men like Tillinghast, men who want to offer you rotten deals. But you don't ever want to take them. Even if it means you have to push a broom for the rest of your life."

Robert looked out at the horizon. Far below them, in the seaport village of Dunwich, the first snowplow was lumbering up Phillips Avenue, carving a path through the town's main thoroughfare. Bewildered gulls circled the sky, searching for roosts that weren't covered with snow.

"It doesn't seem very fair," Robert decided.

"Life's not fair," Mac told him. "But helping Tillinghast makes it worse, not better."

A lone gull hovered in front of them, beating its wings. The poor bird looked exhausted. Robert cleared some snow off the railing so it would have a dry place to rest.

"Could I try your coffee?" he asked.

Mac passed him the cup. "Help yourself."

Robert took a sip and immediately choked on the harsh, bitter flavor. It tasted like he was drinking mud. He spit it out over the side of the balcony.

"This is awful!"

Mac shrugged. "You get used to it."

CHAPTER
EIGHTEEN

Mac and Robert went downstairs and found the rest of the group in the cafeteria: Karina, Lionel, Mrs. Arthur, and even Glenn. He was still wrapped in blankets but was sitting upright at a dining table, surrounded by six different boxes of cereal. He filled a bowl with Cheerios and Raisin Bran and a sprinkle of Mini-Wheats. "Breakfast is all you can eat," he told Robert. "Only the milk's all frozen, so you have to eat it dry."

"You're all right?" Robert asked.

"I'd feel better if I wasn't dressed in a marching band uniform," he said. "Couldn't you find a baseball jersey or something?"

"It was a busy night," Robert said. He noticed his mother hurrying over, so he didn't go into details. "I'll tell you later."

Mrs. Arthur looked panicked. "Have either of you seen Miss Carcasse?" she asked. "I've searched the whole building, but I can't find her anywhere."

Mac had already prepared a story to cover the disappearance. "She stole my keys while we were sleeping," he explained. "She unlocked the door to the gym, and then she went out the front door."

"Why?"

"I'm guessing she tried to walk home."

Mrs. Arthur gasped. "Oh, the poor woman! I knew she wasn't thinking clearly. We have to go find her!"

"There's no way," Mac said. "The snow's covered her tracks. We just have to hope she ended up in a safe place."

"Seems pretty unlikely," Lionel said.

Everyone glared at him, and he gestured to the white drifts piled high against the cafeteria windows. Some of them were five or six feet high. "I mean, look at all that snow. She's probably buried under a ton of that stuff. Frozen like a Popsicle."

"Enough," Mac said. "Show some respect."

Lionel shrugged, poured himself a bowl of Frosted Flakes, and began shoveling cereal into his mouth. "I'm just saying it's her fault for not waiting. I told her my dad would send someone. There's a million users on PerfectPrice who would be happy to come get us."

"No one is coming," Mac insisted. "We're going to eat a big breakfast and then hike into town. I'll pull Glenn on a sled."

"I can walk," Glenn said, standing up and throwing off the blankets to prove his point. "I'll be fine."

Karina, on the other hand, didn't look so sure. She would need an excuse to stay behind when the others left—but what would it be?

They all sat down to a breakfast of dry cereal and peanut butter crackers; all the other cafeteria foods were frozen solid. Glenn's appetite was extraordinary; he consumed five bowls of cereal. Karina explained she was too upset about Miss Carcasse to eat anything. And Lionel continued to insist that hiking into town was a mistake. "We just need to wait a little longer," he told the group. "I promise I can get you all out of here." After several minutes of this argument, Mac became exasperated.

"Look, kid," he said, "your father may be rich, but he's not a genie. He can't move mountains of snow."

"He can do anything," Lionel insisted. "If you'd read the September issue of *Fortune* magazine—"

"I *have* read the September issue," Mac said. "I read all about your father. He lives in New York City, right?"

"That's where his company is," Lionel explained. "He's got five hundred employees. You can't run that kind of business from Dunwich."

"Wait a second," Robert interrupted. "I thought your dad lived in the Heights. How's he going to know about the storm if he lives in New York City?"

"I left him five voicemails," Lionel said. "Obviously he gets thousands of messages, and he can't listen to all of them, but if I leave a bunch, he usually gets back to me."

"So who *do* you live with?" Mrs. Arthur asked.

"My grandma and grandpa. They've got a huge

house, nine bedrooms, with a Jacuzzi and a game room and everything. My new stepmom thought I'd be happier here than in New York." Lionel shrugged. "Which is not true, but my dad agrees with everything she says right now."

"It sounds like a nice house," Robert said, because suddenly he felt like saying something nice. He realized that Mac was right, that maybe he didn't really know Lionel after all.

"Well, I'm sorry, kid," Mac said. "Your father sounds like a very important man, but I'm not going to sit here and wait for him to check his voicemails. We need to leave this school before we all catch pneumonia."

"That's exactly right," Mrs. Arthur said. "We need heat, dry clothes, and shelter. Our bodies can tolerate only so much—"

Suddenly she was interrupted by a low, fluttering noise. At first it sounded like a bicycle tire spinning with a baseball card in the spokes. But the sound grew louder and louder until it shook the room like thunder.

"What is that?" Mrs. Arthur asked.

Mac looked up at the ceiling. "I'm not sure."

"It's coming from outside!" Karina said.

They all ran over to the windows, climbed onto the sill, and peered out over the drifts. The fluttering grew louder still, rattling the glass, shaking clouds of snow from the roof—and then a blue-and-white helicopter soared around the side of the school.

"I knew it!" Lionel shouted. "I told you so!"

CHAPTER
NINETEEN

The chopper disappeared around the side of the building and Lionel ran out of the cafeteria, racing down the central corridor to follow it. His voice was jubilant. "You guys didn't believe me, but I was right all along! PerfectPrice to the rescue!"

Mac ran after him. "Hold up!" he shouted. "Where are you going?"

Robert ran after both of them. Mac was in an all-out sprint, racing to overtake Lionel. Robert didn't understand why until they rounded a corner, moving full speed toward the doors at the end of the east wing.

And then he remembered Tillinghast's instructions: *You'll find an excuse to lead Lionel down this hallway . . .*

the gate will take care of the rest.

But Robert didn't need an excuse.

Lionel was running to the gate on his own.

It was waiting to collect him, invisible to the naked eye, like the unseen strands of a spider's web.

Robert ran faster. He had decided Mac was right, that Lionel didn't deserve to be captured, even if he was mean and spoiled and sometimes very annoying.

"Lionel, wait!" he called.

But Lionel didn't look back and didn't slow down. "They're looking for us," he called back. "I'm going to signal to them!"

"You can't go that way!"

Lionel was nearly at the exit. Robert had no chance of catching him. Mac was closer but still not close enough. Desperate, Mac dove forward, throwing himself at the boy and slamming him face first into a wall of lockers. Lionel missed the gate by inches but Mac couldn't slow himself. He tumbled through the vortex, vanishing from sight, and the gate collapsed around him.

Lionel fell to the floor, covering his face with both hands. Robert knelt down, and Lionel kicked him hard in the shins.

"What'd you do that for?"

"Do what?"

"Tackle me! You nearly broke my nose! Do you want to be rescued or not?"

Robert realized that he and Lionel were alone at the end of an empty hallway. Of course Lionel thought *Robert* had tackled him. Who else could have done it?

Lionel picked himself up off the floor and shoved open the exit doors, climbing over the drifts. Robert lingered in the hallway, staring at the place where the gate had vanished. Things were happening so quickly, he couldn't make sense of them. Where was Mac? Was he really gone?

Robert pushed open the doors and trekked outside into the snow. Lionel was jumping up and down, waving to the helicopter. It was hovering some twenty feet above the ground, slowly descending upon a patch of level ground. The spinning rotors were whipping up snow, and for a moment it looked like the blizzard was raging all over again. Robert had never been so close to a helicopter before. He certainly never thought he'd ever get a chance to ride on one.

Eventually, Mrs. Arthur, Karina, and Glenn caught up with them. "Where's Mac?" Mrs. Arthur asked.

"I don't know," Robert said. He needed more time to think of a better answer to that question.

The pilot left the rotors spinning. He hopped out of the chopper and came running over, a stocky man dressed in an orange jumpsuit.

"Are you folks all right?" he asked, yelling to be heard over the engine.

"We've been better," Mrs. Arthur said. "We lost one of our teachers last night. She wandered into the snow, and we haven't seen her all morning."

"Which one of you is Lionel Quincy?"

"Here," Lionel said, raising his hand.

"All right, Mr. Quincy, I need you to come with me." The pilot looked to Mrs. Arthur. "I'll alert the police to your situation, ma'am. They'll send help as

soon as they can."

Robert's mother blinked. "What about us?"

"This isn't a rescue chopper, ma'am. This is a private commercial aircraft. I've got instructions from PerfectPrice to collect one passenger, Lionel Quincy."

"But we've been trapped here all night—"

"Additional passengers would violate my terms of contract. There are liability issues, you see."

Mrs. Arthur gestured to the helicopter. There were four empty seats inside the cabin. "We haven't had heat all night," she explained. "One of our boys nearly died from exposure. You've got room—"

"She's right," Lionel told the pilot. "We need to bring all of them."

"I have specific instructions," the pilot said.

"But this is an emergency," Lionel said. "These people need our help. I told them all night you were coming."

"I'm sorry, Mr. Quincy, but if I don't honor my PerfectPrice contract, I don't get paid. Now are you coming aboard or not?"

Lionel hesitated. For all of his excitement over the helicopter, it no longer seemed like he wanted to be rescued. But Mrs. Arthur pushed him toward the chopper. "You have to go," she told him. "Your family's waiting for you. We'll be fine."

Lionel followed the pilot to the chopper, climbed aboard, and belted himself into a seat. He didn't look back or say good-bye, but Robert understood that he wasn't being rude; he was simply embarrassed. Being the son of the 87th Most Powerful Titan in the Tech Industry wasn't all it was cracked up to be.

The helicopter rose into the sky, shaking snow from the surrounding trees, and then turned toward town, disappearing over the horizon.

"Well, I guess everybody has a perfect price," Mrs. Arthur said, turning her back on the helicopter. "Isn't that what all their commercials say?"

"Not everybody," Robert said.

Mrs. Arthur went inside to look for Mac, but Robert lingered outside with his friends. He quickly explained what they had just missed, describing how Mac had saved Lionel's life while sacrificing his own.

"Then we have to rescue him," Glenn decided. "We'll cross over, find the urns, open them up, and bring him back."

Karina looked as if she was going to cry. "I'm not sure it's that easy." Then she doubled over in pain, clutching her sides.

"What's wrong?" Robert asked.

She dropped to one knee, head bowed. "I don't know. I don't feel so good."

Robert didn't know it was possible for Karina to feel bad, or to feel anything. She certainly never complained of any pain before. A mild breeze blew past them, shaking snow off the rooftop, and flurries settled all around them.

"Are you okay?" Glenn asked her.

She shook off the pain and stood up. "Yeah, I think so," she said. "Just upset about Mac, that's all."

But she wasn't fine. Something in her face had changed. Her eyes and ears and nose all looked the same, yet something was extraordinarily different.

There were snowflakes in her hair.

And they were starting to melt.

"I'm fine," she said, walking toward the school. "Let's go inside."

"Look down," Robert told her. "Look at your feet."

For the first time in thirty years, she was leaving footprints. Karina gasped. She lifted her right leg and carefully set it down again, like Neil Armstrong taking his first steps on the moon. "Is this for real?"

"You're for real," Robert said.

He suddenly understood that Tillinghast had kept his end of the bargain: a replacement had been delivered through the gate—only it was Mac, not Lionel. And, as promised, Karina's body had been restored.

"Whoa!" Glenn exclaimed. "How did this happen?"

"Mac didn't just rescue Lionel," Robert said. "He rescued Karina, too."

She reached toward the door, pulled on the handle, and laughed with delight when it opened. "Did you see that?" she asked. "Did you see what I did?"

She stepped into the school, leapt toward the ceiling, and whooped when gravity brought her down. She started running, banging her fists on the metal lockers, marveling at the earsplitting racket. She tried doing a cartwheel, tumbled to the floor, picked herself up, and ran some more.

Robert and Glenn stared after her.

"She's lost her mind," Glenn said.

"Can you blame her?" Robert asked.

Pip and Squeak came scampering out of the Music Room, attracted by the sudden commotion. They appeared safe and sound after spending the night inside a trombone.

Karina shrieked with delight, grabbing the rats, spinning them around, and kissing each one on its nose. "You don't know how long I've wanted to do that!"

TWENTY

Even after several minutes of running, leaping, hugging, and shrieking, Karina refused to believe that she was free of Lovecraft Middle School once and for all.

"You're sure I can just walk out of here?" she asked. "Nothing bad's going to happen?"

"We're going to find out," Robert said.

But Karina didn't have any winter clothes, so first they had to raid the school's lost-and-found box. She took her time, matching checkered hats with striped scarves and vice versa, while Pip and Squeak helped her sort the garments into winners and losers.

"Can't you just pick something and get on with it?" Glenn asked.

"I haven't tried on new clothes in thirty years," Karina reminded him. "Let me enjoy this, all right?"

As she sifted through the box, Robert paced in circles. His excitement over Karina's transformation was short-lived. Yes, she was finally free of Tillinghast Mansion—but now what? Where would she live? Who would take care of her? How would she get money for food, clothes, or shelter?

Every time Robert thought he had middle school all figured out, the rules seemed to change and everything got more complicated.

Pip and Squeak came scurrying over and crawled up Robert's leg. *Don't worry*, they told him. *You know what you have to do.* Often the rats would read his thoughts without Robert even realizing it. He scratched his pets behind the ears and then helped them crawl inside his jacket pocket for the long walk home.

Karina emptied the entire lost-and-found box before deciding on a spectacularly mismatched outfit: blue jacket, black scarf, green cap, one left glove, and one right mitten. "And here's my favorite part," she said, plucking

168

orange Garfield earmuffs from the box and placing them on her head. "Are these cool or what?"

"Hey, that reminds me," Glenn said, turning to Robert. "Did you ever give her that card?"

Robert blushed. "No—"

"What card?" Karina asked.

"Robert bought you a valentine. He told me yesterday, when we were out on the ledge. He said that if he fell off the ledge, I was supposed to give it to you."

Karina turned to Robert. "Seriously?"

"It's just Garfield," Robert said. "I know how much you like him—"

"Like him? I love him!"

Robert gave her the envelope. She began to open it, but he stopped her. "Open it later," he said. "Open it when you get home."

The word *home* stopped Karina in her tracks. She suddenly realized she didn't have one. "Where am I going to go?" she asked. "What happens when we get to town?"

"Come on," Robert said. "I have an idea."

They walked outside the school and found Mrs. Arthur peering out across the frozen landscape, dressed in her coat and hat, still searching for Mac. "I can't imagine where he's wandered off to," she said. "It's the weirdest thing. Like he simply vanished."

"Mac's not coming with us," Robert said.

"What do you mean?" Mrs. Arthur asked. "Why not?"

He took a deep breath. "Mac's been captured," he said, and then the whole story came spilling out: "He's imprisoned in Tillinghast Mansion. His soul is trapped in a small ceramic urn, but I think we can rescue him. Yesterday, Glenn and I found chorus robes that will let us sneak into the mansion unnoticed. But first we have to go home, because Karina doesn't have any place to live. She's been trapped here in spirit form for thirty years—"

"Stop," Mrs. Arthur said. "What on earth are you talking about?"

"You're telling it wrong," Karina said. "Start from the beginning. Tell her about your first day of school."

"Yeah," Glenn said, "tell her how you found Pip and Squeak."

"Who?" Mrs. Arthur asked. "What's a Pip and Squeak?"

At the mention of their names, the rats emerged from Robert's coat pocket, twitching their noses, and Mrs. Arthur shrieked.

Collect All Four Terrifying
Volumes in the

LOVECRAFT
MIDDLE SCHOOL

SERIES

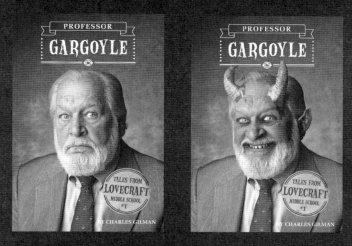

#1 PROFESSOR GARGOYLE

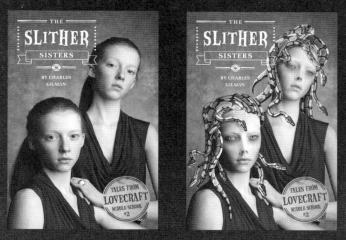

#2 THE SLITHER SISTERS

#3 TEACHER'S PEST

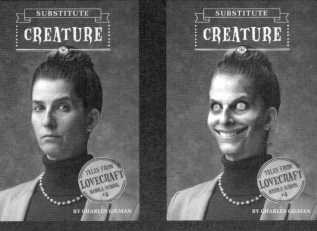

#4 SUBSTITUTE CREATURE

About the Author

Charles Gilman is an alias of Jason Rekulak, an editor who lives in Philadelphia with his wife, Julie, and their children Sam and Anna. When he's not dreaming up new tales of Lovecraft Middle School, he's biking along the fetid banks of the Schuylkill River, in search of two-headed rats and other horrific beasts.

About the Illustrator

From an early age, Eugene Smith dreamed of drawing monsters, mayhem, and madness. Today, he is living the dream in Chicago, where he resides with his wife, Mary, and their daughters Audrey and Vivienne.

Monstrous Thanks

All hail the hard-working folks at Quirk Books, Random House Publisher Services, and National Graphics! Thanks also to Jonathan Pushnik, Deanna Perlmutter, Julie Scott, Roseann Rekulak, West Philly's Green Line Cafe, and Mary Flack.

LOVECRAFT MIDDLE SCHOOL

Is Now Enrolling Students Online!

- **GO** behind the scenes with author Charles Gilman!
- **READ** an interview with illustrator Eugene Smith!
- **DISCOVER** the secrets of the awesome "morphing" cover photograph!
- And much, much more